Heartland™
Love is a Gift

"What is wrong with you? You don't try and join in with anything, you don't want to have anything to do with Lily, you're offhand with Helena when all she tries to do is make you feel like part of the family. You're even being cool towards Dad after he's bent over backwards to make you feel at home here. I just don't understand why you're being like this."

Amy's mouth dropped open. How could Lou be so insensitive to how she was feeling? "Oh, forget it," she said feeling a surge of frustration, "I might have known you wouldn't understand."

"What's that supposed to mean?" Lou snapped.

"Although you might have," Amy continued, "considering how left out you felt when Dad came to stay with us at Heartland!"

There was a long pause. Both sisters stared at each other. "Are you saying that you don't feel as if you fit in?" Lou asked, looking bewildered.

"Yes, Lou, that's exactly how I feel, but don't worry because it won't be long before I'm back at Heartland, where I do!"

Read all the books about Heartland:

www.scholastic.co.uk/zone

Heartland™

Love is a Gift

Lauren Brooke

Scholastic Children's Books,
Euston House, 24 Eversholt Street,
London NW1 1DB, UK
a division of Scholastic Ltd

London ~ New York ~ Toronto ~ Sydney ~ Auckland
Mexico City ~ New Delhi ~ Hong Kong

First published in the UK by Scholastic Ltd, 2004
Series created by Working Partners Ltd

10 digit ISBN 0 439 96868 2
13 digit ISBN 978 0439 96868 3

Printed and bound by Bookmarque Ltd, Croydon, Surrey

6 8 10 9 7

With special thanks to Elisabeth Faith

*For Amber Caravéo — thank you for making Heartland
a special place*

Chapter One

Amy threw the lead rope down on the floor in exasperation. "I don't know what's got into him!" she exclaimed. She glanced across at Ty who was leaning against the fence post, watching. The stallion careered round the paddock with his tail kinked in the air like a banner. Ty tried to look sympathetic but Amy had already caught sight of his grin.

"I'm sorry," Ty apologized, still smiling. "It's just that Dazzle looks as if he's having such a good time. I bet he thinks he's playing tag with you!"

Amy felt a corresponding bubble of laughter well up inside her. It was so good to have Ty back at Heartland, sharing things with her again. Not so long ago he had been in hospital in a coma and Amy had been devastated. Ty was so much more than just the lead stablehand at Heartland. He was Amy's best friend and boyfriend. She pushed a stray strand of hair away from her face before joining Ty at the fence.

Dazzle had paused in his exuberant gallop and was watching them with his ears pricked forward in interest.

"Hey." Ty snapped his fingers. "Earth to Amy."

Amy smiled warmly. "I was just thinking about how good it is to have you home," she said.

"It's nice to know you missed me," Ty replied, smiling back as he went and scooped up the rope from the floor. "Do you want me to try?"

Amy nodded and watched as Ty quietly approached Dazzle with the rope behind his back. The mustang stood still, watching Ty's every movement. Just as Ty drew close enough to reach out with his hand, Dazzle let out a high-pitched squeal and wheeled away. Instead of chasing after the blue roan, Ty immediately turned his back and showed no interest in Dazzle's antics. The stallion bucked several times in high spirits, but Ty resolutely ignored him and so gradually the mustang began to calm down.

Amy smiled to see the puzzled expression on Dazzle's face as he looked across at Ty. Eventually the mustang lowered his head, snorted heavily and made his way over to nuzzle Ty's shoulder. He snorted once more as Ty slowly turned and clipped on his lead rope to walk him to the gate.

"He still responds better to you than to anyone else," Amy commented as they walked into the coolness of the barn. There was a full haynet hanging in the corner of the stall, thoughtfully left there by Ben, the stablehand at Heartland.

"He'd just tired himself out and was finally ready to come in," Ty replied, slipping off Dazzle's headcollar.

But Amy knew that there was an extra special bond between Ty and the mustang. "Ben's already prepared the evening feeds, so all we need to do is give them out and we're done," she declared.

Ty straightened up. "Terrific," he replied.

Just then they heard Lou, Amy's sister, calling from the yard. "Amy, can you come in when you've got a second?"

"You go," Ty told Amy. "I'll finish up here. There's not much left to do."

"Are you sure?" Amy frowned. She didn't want Ty to overdo things so soon after his time in hospital.

"Go on. It might be important," he said, leaning forward to kiss Amy on the forehead. "I'll see you in the morning."

"Thanks, Ty," Amy said gratefully, and patted Dazzle before slipping from the stall.

Lou and Scott were sitting at the kitchen table with Jack Bartlett, the girls' grandfather. Amy kicked off her shoes as she walked in and noted with surprise that her sister didn't automatically tell her to put them away.

Amy smiled a welcome to Scott, Lou's boyfriend and the vet for Heartland. He and Lou had been dating for a while now. She glanced at Lou who was sitting alongside him and immediately noticed an air of excitement surrounding her normally calm sister. "What's happening?" Amy asked curiously.

"Well," Lou began, "do you think you could manage without

me for a couple of weeks?" Her blue eyes shone as she reached across the table to put her hand over Scott's. "Scott is flying out to Australia for a conference in a couple of weeks – and he wants me to go with him."

"For a few weeks!" Amy exclaimed in surprise.

"Well, it's going to be a little over that by the time you add in the travelling," Lou admitted. "The conference lasts for five days but as it's in Australia I thought we might visit Daddy. I rang him today and he's invited me to stay with him, Helena and the baby while Scott is at the conference. Then, when Scott's free, we thought we'd take a holiday together before heading home," she explained, excitement in her voice.

Amy thought it over. When their mom had died in a tragic accident, Lou had given up her banking job in the city and moved to Heartland to take over the business side of things, leaving Amy free to work with the abused and neglected horses they took in. Now, the thought of losing her sister for a month suddenly made Amy realize just how big a part of Heartland Lou had become.

"Amy?" Lou prompted gently, and Amy could tell by the way the excitement had left her sister's eyes that this wasn't the reaction she had been hoping for.

She took a deep breath and forced herself to smile. "That's great news, Lou. Of course you should go. You deserve a break after all the hard work you've put in here."

Lou looked delighted. She pushed her chair back and hurried round the table to give Amy a hug. "Are you sure you can spare me?"

Amy pushed down the mixed feelings that were whirling round in her stomach and hugged her sister back. She was genuinely pleased that the opportunity had come along for Lou – but she was going to miss her. "Sure, I'm sure."

Scott cleared his throat and said, "I've arranged for a locum with a very good reputation to come and look after the practice while we're away."

Amy smiled across at him as Lou added, "And I'll make sure all the paperwork's completely up to date. You shouldn't have too much to do while I'm away. You'll just have to remember to pay all the bills at the end of the month, check our email every day and—"

"Enough, enough," Jack broke in, laughing. "I'm sure you'll leave detailed instructions for everything – and instructions on how to follow the instructions! Amy, I've promised that I'll cover most of Lou's work for her – you have enough to do as it is."

"Thanks, Grandpa. I'm sure that between us we'll manage," Amy replied, smiling.

"That's terrific," said Lou, "I'll call Daddy back and say yes to his invitation. Thanks so much Amy, Grandpa," she looked from one to the other. "You've got no idea what this means to me."

It suddenly hit Amy that Lou would be spending a fair amount of time with their father in Australia – time that she would have loved to share with them. It was difficult not to let her feelings show as Lou began to punch their father's number into the phone. Quietly she slid her feet into her boots and slipped back out into the yard.

When Amy let herself into Sundance's stall, her pony looked up from his haynet and nickered softly. "Oh, Sundance," Amy whispered, tangling her fingers in his mane. She leaned against his warm golden neck as familiar feelings of loss swept over her. She was thrilled that Lou was going to Australia – her sister deserved a holiday and Amy knew how much the chance to spend time with their father would mean to her. But Lou's announcement had disturbed the precarious sense of security that Amy had gradually built after her mother's death.

An unwelcome image flashed into her head – the darkness of the storm, the tree falling on to the car, the terrible blackness before waking up in hospital to be told by Lou that their mom was dead. She gave a deep sigh. *Whenever I think I'm handling things since Mom died, something happens to make me realize that I'm not dealing with it as well as I thought. I still miss her so much.* Sundance's ears flickered back towards Amy. He turned his head and lipped gently at her hair. Amy leaned against the pony, drawing comfort from his warmth and strength.

"I thought I might find you here. You always come out to the horses when you have some thinking to do," Jack said quietly, looking over the stall door.

Amy turned to stare at him.

What's on your mind?" he asked, his blue eyes showing concern.

Amy hesitated and straightened Sundance's forelock. "I guess I'm not a hundred per cent sure how I feel about Lou leaving," she admitted.

"You wish you were going, too?" Jack inquired, sympathetically.

Amy patted Sundance's shoulder before joining her grandfather at the door. "I would love to see Dad again," she agreed. "But, more than that, I've suddenly realized how much I've come to need Lou."

"I know," Jack said and squeezed her arm reassuringly. "And I bet Lou would understand. You should go and talk to her."

Lou looked up from where she was rinsing cups at the sink as Amy walked in.

"Has Scott gone?" Amy asked.

"Yes, he's got an awful lot to organize before we fly out," Lou replied as she wiped her hands dry. "But I'm glad we've got a minute to talk. I want to make sure that you really are OK about this trip, now that you've had a chance to think about it. Earlier I had the feeling that you weren't being completely open about how you felt."

"I am pleased for you," Amy reassured her quickly. "It's just that it won't seem so much like home with you gone. And, I know it's selfish, but I so wish I could go, too. I'd love to see Dad."

Lou looked a little upset. "I guessed you might be feeling like that," she said quietly.

"I don't want you to worry," Amy went on, pulling out a chair and sitting down at the table. "I think it's great that you're getting this chance to go – I really do. What did Dad say when you spoke to him?"

"He was pleased," Lou replied, joining Amy at the table. "He said he'd be in touch again soon to sort out the final arrangements — and he sent you his love."

Amy smiled. It was only recently that she had begun to get to know her father, Tim Fleming. He had left the family after a bad show-jumping accident had left him traumatized. Amy had only been three at the time, and she hadn't seen Tim since his accident — until a couple of months ago. During his brief stay at Heartland, Amy and her father had, to her surprise, bonded well. Unfortunately, Lou, who being older had had more time to develop a close relationship with their father before his accident, had found it harder to bond with Tim again. Now Amy hoped that, on this trip, Lou would be able to regain the closeness she had shared with her father in her childhood. Since Tim now lived in Australia, with his new wife and baby daughter, it wasn't often that Amy or Lou had an opportunity to spend time with him.

"Why don't you take some photos of yourself, and the rest of us, working at Heartland?" Lou suggested. "That way I can take them with me. I'll make sure I take lots of photos when I'm at Dad's ranch — of him and Helena and their baby, Lily. I know it won't be the same, but…" her voice tailed off helplessly.

"That's a great idea," said Amy quickly. She grinned. "Just don't forget to take snaps of every single one of Dad's horses."

"Ah," Lou nodded, smiling back. "We wouldn't want you to miss out on the really important aspect of the trip!"

* * *

Early the next morning, Amy pulled on her clothes and headed out to feed the horses. She was just mixing the last bucket when Ty arrived. "You must have been up even earlier than usual," he commented, glancing at his watch.

"I didn't sleep much," Amy replied.

"You're often up and doing things before I get here lately," Ty frowned. "You do too much already, without taking on extra work."

Amy looked away, not wanting to catch his eye. The truth was that she had been trying to lighten Ty's workload since he had returned to Heartland after leaving hospital. Ty had been badly injured and left in a coma after a twister struck Heartland and brought the roof beams of the old barn crashing down on top of him. But Amy knew that Ty was too proud to accept help, and so she had tried not to draw attention to what she was doing. In an effort to change the subject, she quickly explained what had happened the previous evening. Ty agreed that the photos were a good idea.

"I thought I'd take a few shots of the horses while they're feeding, and then some of you and Ben turning them out in the paddocks," Amy told him.

Ben's horse, Red, was looking over his stable door, eagerly anticipating his morning feed, which Amy delivered. "Then if you could take some of me working with Dazzle in the ring," she went on, "it will give Helena a good idea of what goes on during a typical day at Heartland."

"Is there such a thing?" Ty joked, picking up a grooming kit.

"Morning!" Ben called as he arrived on the yard.

"Hi, Ben," Ty called back. Then he winked at Amy. "I'd better get going. We want all the horses to look their best for their Australian cousins now, don't we?"

"Australia? Have I missed something?" Ben asked, looking confused.

"Lots!" Amy laughed. "But I don't have time to explain now. I've got some photos to take."

After Amy had taken snapshots of Ben and Ty at work, Ty took the camera and Amy led Dazzle into the ring. Dazzle was a mustang stallion that had come to Heartland while Ty was still in a coma. Amy hadn't connected as well as she had hoped with the beautiful roan, but the horse had developed a special bond with Ty when he had come out of hospital. Since the wild mustang had responded so quickly to Ty, Amy had suggested that he do most of the work with the horse.

Now Amy was beginning to do more work with Dazzle herself. "Here we go, boy," said Amy, stopping in the middle of the ring and unclipping the lead rein. Dazzle snorted loudly as she drove him away from her, to the outside of the ring, and then sent him cantering freely round the perimeter. Amy knew it wouldn't be long before the stallion showed signs of wanting to join-up with her. She was gradually gaining his trust now, and she knew that each time they completed a join-up, the bond between them grew. Watching the stallion eat up the ground with his long stride, his tail streaming out behind him, Amy felt a rush of pride. She forgot about Ty and the photos; all her concentration was focused on the beautiful stallion who was now asking to join-up with her. He had lowered his head and was opening and closing his mouth, waiting for Amy to allow him to cross the ring and be with her.

Amy deliberately dropped her aggressive stance, turned her body sideways to the horse and waited. Dazzle slowed to a stop and Amy could sense him watching at her. The hairs on the back of her neck tingled as she waited for him to approach. Slowly, Dazzle crossed the ring and came to a halt beside Amy, blowing deeply on her shoulder. Amy raised her hand and gently rubbed his nose. Then she took a few steps forward and, as if they were bound by an invisible thread, Dazzle followed her. Wherever Amy went, the mustang walked patiently behind, showing her the utmost trust and respect.

With the session ended, Ty walked over and snapped Dazzle's lead rein back on. "He's really beginning to respond to you," Ty enthused, leading Dazzle out of the ring. "I think I got some great pictures. Looking at him now, there's no way anyone would guess how wild he once was."

Amy nodded and patted Dazzle's warm neck. "He's still got a way to go, but he's coming on well. And most of that's down to you," she added. Then she glanced across at Ty and noticed that his face had suddenly lost its colour. "Are you OK?" she asked anxiously.

"Sure," Ty replied. "Don't worry so much. I'm fine."

"Well, you look tired," said Amy stubbornly. "You should take a break. I'll rub Dazzle down."

"Trust me, I'm OK," Ty insisted, and clicked to Dazzle to follow him into the barn.

"Ty," Amy called after him, but he didn't turn back. Amy sighed. He was determined to do everything for himself, she realized. From now on, when she was trying to help, she'd have to be less obvious about it.

The next week was filled with Lou's preparations to leave. Despite Amy and Grandpa's constant reassurances that they knew what to do in her absence, Lou was determined to leave Heartland as well organized as possible.

Amy was busy sweeping the yard when she heard the kitchen door fly open. Looking up, she saw Lou running over to her, flapping a large white envelope. Amy stared in surprise.

"Look at this," Lou said. "It's for you. I think it's from Dad."

Puzzled, Amy took the envelope and opened it. Her grey eyes widened as she scanned the letter. "You're right, it is from Dad," she said slowly. "He wants me to come out to Australia with you and Scott!"

Lou gasped. "He didn't say anything about it to me. He must have wanted it to be a surprise," she said in delight.

Amy re-read the letter again — more slowly this time.

Dear Amy,

I know that by now Lou will have told you of her plans to come out to Australia. The time that you and I spent together on my last visit was very special and it would mean a great deal to me if you could come out with Lou. We could spend longer with one another this time — my last stay was too short. Helena says she looks forward to getting to know you both — and introducing you to your baby sister, of course! I know that it won't be easy for you to leave Heartland, but promise you'll try to come? I want to show you my current stock of sports horses and I have told everyone here about your "special touch". I won't be the only one disappointed if you don't make it!

Please pass on my regards to Jack and tell Lou that we are looking forward to seeing her and Scott. I'm also looking forward to riding out with her; I know she's been practising since my last visit! I'm enclosing an open air ticket for you and hope you will be able to use it.

All my love,
Daddy.

"This is wonderful!" Lou's eyes shone. "We can get to know our half-sister together. You'll love being at Daddy's ranch — spending time with him and seeing all his horses…"

Her voice trailed off as Amy looked up, slowly shaking her head. "It's no good, Lou. We can't both leave Heartland. I just can't go."

Chapter 2

Amy hitched the halter further over her shoulder as she walked down to the paddock with her best friend, Soraya. Even the sight of her pony, Sundance, standing at the gate did little to lift her spirits.

"Why don't you at least try to work out if there's any way you could go and leave things here?" Soraya suggested.

"There's just no point," Amy sighed, pushing a strand of hair out of her eyes. "I couldn't leave Ty and Ben to do all the work on their own."

Soraya flipped her black curly hair over her shoulder and walked across to Jasmine, one of the long-term residents at Heartland. Jasmine was an ex-dressage pony, about to be destroyed due to lameness when Amy's mom had rescued her and successfully treated her so that she could be used for light work. Soraya slipped the halter on the pretty, dished-faced pony and clicked to her to fall into step beside Amy and Sundance. Amy's buckskin pony swished his tail in annoyance and laid his ears back, rolling the whites of his eyes dramatically.

"Stop it!" said Amy, for once the bad-tempered antics of Sundance failing to amuse her. Sundance was clearly so surprised at being spoken to sharply by Amy, who was the one person he adored, that he lowered his head submissively and walked quietly beside her.

Soraya laughed. "I've never seen him so well behaved," she said. "Perhaps you should tell him off more often."

Amy immediately felt awful. "Sorry, boy," she murmured, patting his neck. Sundance snorted and gave her a sharp nudge with his nose that made her smile.

Once they had tacked up and were clattering out of the yard towards the sandy track that would take them up Teak's Hill, Amy felt her spirits lift. It seemed as if Sundance sensed her mood because he did everything with more enthusiasm than usual – as if he was trying to cheer her up. He galloped faster, jumped higher and felt lighter than ever before.

"Wow!" Soraya gasped as they pulled up for a rest. "What's got into him today? The way he cleared that fallen tree should qualify him for High Prelim, at least!"

Amy grinned, and as they headed for home, she began to think over Soraya's earlier suggestion of finding a way to leave Heartland. After riding in silence for a while, she turned to Soraya. "I just don't see how Grandpa and the boys could manage without me for so long. A week, yes, but not a month. It just wouldn't be fair. We couldn't afford to hire a temporary stablehand and Ty still needs to take things easy after his accident. There's no way he could take on my work on top of what he's doing already."

"I wouldn't mind coming up and helping for a couple of hours each day," Soraya offered generously.

Amy considered her offer for a moment before shaking her head regretfully. "Thanks, that's really kind of you, but there's just so much to do. Morning feeds, turning out, exercising, working with the horses, mucking out the stalls, cleaning tack, bedding down for the night, evening feeds and then trying to keep the yard tidy." She looked across at her friend and grinned. "Wow, I didn't realize how hard I work."

Soraya smiled in return. "I know I couldn't put in the hours that you do, but I'd still be able to take on some of the stable work. If you ask me, you need a holiday – particularly with everything you've been through lately."

Amy sank into thought. The last few months had been pretty tough, with sickness among the horses and the tornado that had ripped through the farm causing Ty's accident. "I would love to go," she admitted to her friend. "But Heartland comes first," she added firmly.

"I know," Soraya nodded her head, looking serious. "But I think it's time you admitted that the problem isn't so much how we would all cope without you, but how you would cope being without us!" She broke into a wide grin as Amy pretended to take a swat at her before shortening her reins and cantering back to the yard.

Amy waved Soraya off and she turned to walk back to the farmhouse. To her surprise, she found Ty, Ben, Lou and Grandpa all together in the yard. Amy raised her eyebrows questioningly at Ty.

"We've been talking and we've decided that you're going to Australia," he announced with a grin, getting straight to the point.

Amy sighed, "I'd love to go, but it's just not fair. It's too much work for you all to manage with both Lou and me away."

Ben stepped forward and Amy could see concern in his eyes. "Spending some time with your dad and his new family is too important for anything else to get in the way, Amy – even Heartland." Amy knew where he was coming from. Ben had missed out on a relationship with his mother for six years and he was talking from hard experience.

"I know, Ben," she said, biting her lip. "But—"

"How would you feel if we could get someone else to work here while you're away?" Lou interrupted.

Amy looked from one face to the next and suddenly realized that they all knew something she didn't. She thought quickly, and then her grey eyes widened with excitement. "Marnie!" she breathed.

Lou nodded, her blue eyes dancing.

"But for several weeks?" she questioned.

"I was talking with her not long ago and she mentioned that her job in the city was really getting on top of her. She was thinking of putting in for a leave of absence just to get away from it all for a while. I suddenly realized this morning that she might like the idea of coming to stay here. She's always loved helping out and she knows the stable routine. So I called her while you were out riding and she jumped at the chance." Lou explained. "At least think about it, Amy," she urged.

Just for a moment, Amy felt excitement well up inside her at the thought of going to Australia. "I'll give it some thought," she said and before anyone could say any more, she slipped away into the tack room. She felt so torn. She would love to go to Australia with Lou, but then she knew that she would worry about Ty and Heartland and that could end up spoiling her stay – which wouldn't be fair on Lou or her father.

"Hey," Ty's voice broke into Amy's thoughts. He sat down beside her on a storage trunk. "You know you'll regret it if you don't go," he pointed out.

"I have thought it through," said Amy quietly. "And it's not just the extra work you would all have to do if I wasn't here. I'm also worried that I might get in the way of Dad and Lou."

"What?" Ty looked puzzled.

"The last time Dad visited, I got to spend a lot of time with him and work through a lot of my hang-ups. But Lou didn't really get close to him – not in the way that she'd hoped. I think that if they have this time together in Australia, she'll be able to build a better relationship with him – and that's so important to her. She used to be so close to Dad when she was younger, living in England. I think it hit her really hard when he came to stay and they didn't jump straight back into their old relationship."

"But, Amy, you're not really allowing yourself to see the whole picture," Ty replied gently. "All you've done is worry about the horses, worry about me, and worry about Lou and your father. Now how about taking a good look at all the good that can be achieved if you go?"

Amy stared at him.

"Don't think I haven't noticed that ever since I got out of hospital you've been doing half my work for me," Ty continued. "It's time you let me get back into it. You have to trust my judgement on this, Amy." He looked intently at her. "Heartland's been a little quieter than usual so that the repairs could take place after the storm. They're done now, Candy's ready to go and Dazzle actually works better with me than he does with you."

Amy nodded. She knew it was true.

"We can manage here, with Marnie's help, and it's important for you to spend time with your father and meet your other sister. Just think things through fully before you finally make up your mind, OK?" Ty finished.

Amy thought about Ty's words and realized that everything he said made perfect sense. Heartland really would be fine with Ty in charge and the extra help from Marnie. Her heart began to soar as it dawned on her that there was nothing to prevent her from going to Australia!

Amy let herself into the kitchen where Lou, Jack, Ben and Ty were sitting round the table. Lou looked up with a hopeful expression in her eyes. "Well?" she asked.

Amy suddenly couldn't think of a single thing to say.

Grandpa laughed. "Now that Amy's had every argument taken away from her, I'm starting to believe she doesn't actually want to go to Australia," he teased.

"Are you kidding?" Amy exclaimed. "I mean it's not like I won't miss you guys," she said, glancing across into Ty's green eyes. "And the horses especially," she added.

"Gee thanks," Ben joked.

"You know what I mean," Amy told him, running one hand

through her long brown hair. "But getting to see Daddy again, and look over his ranch? And work with all his horses? I mean, wow!"

"It's supposed to be a holiday," Ty reminded her gently and everyone laughed. Lou called to Amy above the noise, "So I guess this means you're going then?"

"You bet!" Amy replied happily, as Ty crossed over to where she stood and hugged her.

Lou chewed the end of her pencil and looked again at her notepad. "There's still a fair bit to organize before we fly out tomorrow. Have you packed yet?"

Amy nodded. "All done." She had packed a large rucksack the previous evening. "And I've called Dad, to tell him when we'll arrive."

"What did he say?" Lou asked, looking up.

"He said that he'd drive out himself to pick us up from the airport. Actually, we didn't get the chance to say much; the baby was crying and it was difficult to talk."

"Lily," Lou corrected.

Amy didn't reply. It had felt weird talking to her father with his new daughter making her presence so loudly felt. She couldn't really get her head round the fact that their father had three daughters now. Even though they had been apart for most of her life, she still thought of it as only Lou and herself who belonged to him.

Lou didn't seem to have any such hang-ups. "I can't wait to meet her," she enthused. "Just think, a new sister!"

"Half-sister," Amy murmured.

Lou returned to her list, a frown creasing her forehead. "I've ordered the food, paid this month's bills," she muttered, ticking things off on her list.

"We need the farrier to come and trim Sugarfoot and Dazzle's feet," Amy reminded her.

As Lou reached for the phone, Amy slipped from the room, keen to get in a final join-up session with Dazzle.

That evening Grandpa cooked a farewell meal for them all. As Amy looked round the table at the people she loved, she realized that she couldn't have chosen a better way to spend her final evening in at home. Her feelings of excitement seemed to be infectious – everyone chatted noisily about the trip to Australia.

Later on, Amy walked with Ty to his truck. "I'm really going to miss you, Ty," she said quietly.

"Me, too," he replied turning to her. "But it's not often that you'll get this kind of an opportunity."

Amy chewed her lower lip. Secretly she was still worried about leaving Ty. There were times when he looked pale at the end of a day's work, even though he never complained.

Ty clearly read her mind. "You'll never get any enjoyment from this trip if you spend all of your time worrying about things here," he told her gently.

"I'm sorry," Amy smiled. "I just feel guilty about leaving when you need a holiday more than I do."

Ty pretended to look stern. "Enough! Now, promise you'll email," he said.

Amy laughed. "I promise," she replied. "And you've got to email and let me know everything that's happening here."

"I will," Ty assured her. "Whenever I can grab a minute!" He kissed her gently, and held her for a moment longer than usual before climbing into his truck.

As Amy watched Ty's truck disappearing down the drive, Lou called from the kitchen, interrupting her thoughts. "Amy, don't forget we've got an early start tomorrow," she pointed out. And, despite her worries, Amy couldn't help but feel a thrill of excitement. Within twenty-four hours, she would see her father!

Amy was up very early the next morning. She hadn't been able to sleep well. She was too excited. She pulled on her yard clothes and hurried outside, intending to do as much work as she could before leaving. Rising before it was even light also meant she would have some time on her own with the horses to make her goodbyes.

First she decided to collect the haynets from the stalls and fill for the evening. She figured it would make Marnie's first day a little easier. As she walked towards the stable block, the horses stirred restlessly in their deep straw beds and a few put their heads out over their doors. They blinked at her in surprise and nickered gently. They weren't used to being disturbed so early. "Go back to sleep," Amy whispered, kissing velvety noses as she slipped from one stall to the next.

Then she spent the next hour and a half cleaning and filling water buckets, mixing feeds and grooming. As she body-brushed each of the horses with long, firm strokes, she told them where she was going, promising that she wouldn't be gone long.

As daylight flooded over the farm, its brightness reflecting off the white boards of the farmhouse, Ty and Ben arrived.

"What are you doing out here?" Ben asked, shaking his head in mock disapproval.

"Oh, you know, just saying goodbye to the horses and telling them to behave themselves while I'm away," Amy smiled.

"OK, and what's left for us to do?" Ty asked, lifting one eyebrow and looking at her quizzically.

"You just need to turn them out," Amy admitted, holding up her hands and laughing. "I'll go in and get ready in a moment. I just want to say one last goodbye." She fished a horse cookie from her pocket.

Sundance whinnied as Amy approached, tossing his head up and down, making his golden mane bounce. "How is it that you always know when there's a treat on the horizon?" Amy laughed as Sundance pushed at her hands. "There you go, greedy!"

Sundance crunched happily on the cookie while Amy rubbed him gently between the eyes. Her heart swelled with love for the little pony that her mom had bought for her. "Be a good boy," she told him. "Don't boss the others around too much, stay out of trouble and try not to be greedy."

Sundance snorted, sounding exactly as if he was laughing at Amy's request.

She kissed him affectionately before hurrying away, reminding herself that it wouldn't be long before she was be back. She hadn't realized just how difficult leaving would be.

"Amy!" cried Lou in exasperation as Amy hurried into the farmhouse. "We're going in ten minutes and just look at you!" Amy looked down guiltily at her stained yard clothes and her dirty hands. "I'll be ready," she promised. "I just need to shower and change out of these clothes. My bags are already at the bottom of the stairs."

Lou reached over and plucked a piece of straw from Amy's hair. "I bet you haven't even had breakfast."

"I can grab something at the airport," Amy called over her shoulder and headed for the door.

Amy had pulled on a clean white T-shirt and was tucking it into a pair of jeans when she heard Scott's truck pull into the yard. Looking out of the window she saw a slim, blonde-haired girl get out of the passenger side. Scott had picked Marnie up from the bus station earlier. Lou had suggested that she leave her car back in the city and use the Heartland truck at the farm.

Pushing her feet into a pair of sneakers, Amy pulled a comb through her long hair and tied it back into a ponytail. She glanced at her reflection in the mirror. Her cheeks were flushed and her grey eyes sparkled back at her. Grabbing her jacket from the chair, she ran down the stairs two at a time and arrived in the yard just as Scott was loading the last of the bags into the truck. "All set?" he asked. "Got your passport?"

Amy double-checked her back pocket and nodded before turning to greet Marnie.

"Hi Amy!" Marnie exclaimed. "It's great to be back at

Heartland again. Although I'll miss seeing you and Lou, of course."

"Thanks so much for coming to help out," said Amy, giving her a hug.

Marnie hugged her back. "No problem. You have a good time, you hear? And no worrying about what's going on here — we're going to look after everything."

Amy turned to Grandpa who was holding the door of the truck open for her. "Goodbye, Grandpa," she said.

"Bye honey. You call us as soon as you reach Tim and Helena's, OK?" he told her before wrapping her in a huge bear hug.

"We will, first thing," she promised, hugging him fiercely before standing back so Lou could do the same.

Ben, who was driving them to the airport, climbed into the driver's seat and turned on the engine. Amy went to Ty who was standing quietly nearby.

"Take care," he said and, aware of everybody's eyes on them, he hugged her briefly. "Email, OK?" he whispered.

Amy nodded and laughed. "Soraya's told me she expects at least three emails a day," she said. "What with writing to all of you, I probably won't have time to see Dad, never mind any of his horses!"

Ben beeped the horn and Amy saw that Lou and Scott were already in the truck — Lou in the back, Scott in the front next to Ben. Lou's fair head was close to Scott's dark one as she leaned forward from the back seat to whisper something in Scott's ear.

"Take care," Amy said quietly, looking up into Ty's emerald

green eyes. "I'll email the first chance I get and I'll call, I promise." Then, before she could give in to the tears that were prickling the backs of her eyes, she ran across to the truck and climbed in alongside her sister. Lou stopped chatting excitedly with Scott and gave Amy a wide grin.

Ben let out the clutch and the truck picked up speed as it moved down the long drive that led away from the farmhouse, past the paddocks on either side. Lou and Amy turned back and waved furiously until the three figures were out of sight.

"I can't believe that we're finally on our way!" Lou said, reaching over and squeezing Amy's hand.

Amy felt a sharp pang at leaving Heartland, but then she began to feel the same butterflies in her stomach that she always had before a competition. "Australia!" she declared aloud. "Here we come!"

Chapter Three

"I wonder what Dad's ranch will look like?" said Lou excitedly as the plane came in to land.

Amy pictured strings of beautiful sport horses being ridden out for exercise. "I imagine it will be very professional," she mused.

"Amy!" Lou laughed. "I was thinking of Dad and Helena's house, not the stables!"

Amy caught her sister's eye and laughed in return. As usual, all her thoughts had been on the horses.

The journey to Sydney, Australia, had involved several changes and lots of sitting around and waiting for flights. Amy had spent the time in airports chatting with Lou and Scott and flicking through magazines. While she was actually in the air, she had kept herself entertained watching a couple of the in-flight movies and, having hardly slept the night before, she found it easy to catch up on missed sleep, too.

Nevertheless, it had been a very long journey and, by the time the plane eventually landed, Amy was almost bursting with the need to be off and away to her father's ranch – which she knew was several hours' drive from Sydney.

When they finally had their bags and got through customs, Amy hurried in front of Lou and Scott, who were strolling along happily hand in hand, and searched the collected crowd of friends and relatives for her father.

She spotted him almost at once. He was looking around for his daughters, and when he saw Amy, a delighted expression broke out on his tanned face.

"Dad!" Amy called and hurried over to her father, her heart skipping with excitement. She meant to hug him, but when she reached him she suddenly felt a little awkward. She had forgotten how tall her father was. Tim didn't seem to notice, though, and he caught her up in an enthusiastic embrace.

"Amy," she heard him murmur against her hair before he released her to greet Lou and Scott. Amy smiled at the sight of her sister's golden head pressed against her father's dark curly hair – Lou had inherited her colouring from their mother. Amy couldn't help picturing how Marion and Tim must have looked together.

Tim bent down to pick up two dark blue suitcases. "Both of my girls here – I can't believe it," he said, giving them a wink.

Lou and Amy looked at one another and smiled. Amy's heart skipped, they were a family again – even if it was just for a short while – and she was going to make the most of it.

As they drove away from the airport in his Land Cruiser, Tim immediately began discussing the details of their visit.

"Helena wanted me to let you know that she would have come to meet you, but she was anxious to make sure everything was ready for your stay," Tim told them in his strong English accent that was so similar to Lou's. "She was baking a chocolate cake big enough to feed us all for a week when I left." He changed gears and accelerated on to the highway. "My team at the ranch are looking forward to meeting you both. And they've heard all about your healing touch, Amy." His grey eyes met Amy's in the rear-view mirror.

"I just listen to the horses, that's all," Amy replied shyly, but she couldn't help feeling pleased at his words.

"How many people do you have helping out on the ranch, Dad?" Lou asked.

"Sam's my manager and my right-hand man. I couldn't run the place without him," Tim explained. "Then there's Pat who does all the running about for us, collecting horses when Sam or I can't, seeing to the deliveries and maintaining the grounds. Last but by no means least, there's my team of eight stablehands who train the young horses I buy. Those eight look after three horses each.

"So you have twenty-four horses then?" Amy commented.

"Twenty-six at the moment," Tim corrected her. There are two that I look after myself. I really want you to meet them, Amy."

"Why those two especially?" she asked curiously.

"Ah, all will be revealed," he replied.

"Is Lily saying her first words yet, Daddy?" Lou asked with interest, changing the subject.

"She's making a lot of noise from dawn 'til dusk," her father chuckled. "She reminds me a lot of how you were at that age. She's crawling now and using me as a climbing frame at every opportunity."

Amy watched her sister's expression soften.

"Mum said that I never left you alone," Lou remarked.

"Neither does Lily," Tim replied. "Not that I'm complaining."

Amy sat quietly, trying to make sense of the unsettled feeling that was creeping over her. It was difficult listening to her father reminisce about his time with Lou, and now with Lily, when she had spent most of her childhood apart from him.

Tim turned to Scott who was sat alongside him in the front of the car and changed the subject. They began to discuss Scott's schedule. He'd be staying just the one evening with them before travelling out to his conference, which was a three-hour drive away. He was staying there for the five days of the conference before coming back to pick up Lou for their holiday. "I hear that you're going to be listening to various lectures on non-invasive therapies, but which aspect of it are you most interested in?" Tim asked.

Scott, who was keenly interested in alternative remedies, especially when used in conjunction with conventional methods, responded with enthusiasm. "All of it, I guess! Laser treatment, MRI, magnetic and ultrasound therapy – it all fascinates me."

While Scott spoke, Amy couldn't help but notice the pride in Lou's eyes as she listened. Amy felt a rush of pleasure for her sister, mixed with a sudden longing to see Ty. *I guess he's sleeping now*, she thought. She knew that Virginia was eight hours behind in time and it was eight o' clock now in Australia.

"Not long now," Tim suddenly announced. They had been driving for quite some time along a stretch of road with huge wheat fields on either side for as far as the eye could see. He indicated right and turned the Land Cruiser on to a smaller road.

Amy felt excitement rise up through her stomach as round the corner a long, low building came into sight. It was a white, boarded house with a veranda running along the length of it.

"Dad, it's lovely!" Lou exclaimed.

Amy wound down her window and leaned out, her long brown hair whipping behind in the breeze. A little way from the ranch stood a pristine stable block. The closer they got to the ranch, the more it looked like something out of a horse magazine. Unlike Heartland, which was compact and homely, her father's yard obviously operated on a much larger scale. Amy could see figures moving about and two large horses tied to the wall.

They began driving slowly past white-railed paddocks where horses grazed the lush grass. Amy ran an experienced eye over the animals and was surprised at the differences between some of them. Most of the horses were fit and lean with a healthy shine to their coats. There were a few, however, which were clearly not one hundred per cent fit.

"We have a few new arrivals," Tim explained, as if he knew what she was thinking. "They'll spend the next twelve months being backed and given basic training because when we buy them in, they're raw, unpolished youngsters. By the time they leave, they're fit, disciplined and displaying top potential."

Amy recognized the mixture of pride and satisfaction in her father's voice. It was exactly how she sounded whenever she talked about the work they did at Heartland.

"What kind of time scale do you work to?" Amy asked, interested because at Heartland they never put any time limit on a horse's rehabilitation. There was no pressure. Each horse was treated as an individual, which didn't include running to a schedule.

"We give them a week to settle in, just being handled each day. Then, in the next few weeks, we lunge and long-rein. The next stage is to introduce them to a bridle and saddle before backing them," her father told her. "Then they go to school and get down to the real stuff of training. Flat work, followed by jumping and, in the final stages of their time here, some experience on the show circuit. It not only increases their confidence and gives them a starting history for buyers, it also gets them known to the type of people we want to sell to."

"It seems very comprehensive," Lou said, sounding impressed. "I'd love to see the way you've got things set up while I'm here, if that's OK, Dad."

"Sure," Tim responded, pleased.

Amy wasn't really interested in the financial side of her father's business, but she was keen to get to know the horses. "What are the names of the horses you have at the moment, Dad?" she asked quickly, before Lou could start talking finance and statistics.

"Well, if you don't mind waiting a little while longer, I'll introduce you to each one personally," Tim said, smiling. Clearly he understood exactly how impatient Amy was feeling!

With a smooth crunch on the gravel outside the ranch, the Land Cruiser drew to a halt. Scott, who had fallen asleep during the journey, blinked his eyes and stretched.

As she climbed out of the car, Amy noticed a woman standing on the veranda, holding a baby in her arms. It had to be Helena. As Amy looked across at the attractive brunette, she couldn't help feeling a sense of relief that Helena looked nothing like her own mom had.

Helena's face broke into a smile as she made her way down the steps and walked over to greet them. "It's so lovely to meet you at last," she said warmly. "Tim has been longing to get you over here."

Tim stepped forward and formally introduced them all before scooping Lily out of Helena's arms. "This is Lily," he said proudly, looking down at the baby who was chuckling and pulling his hair. "Lily, these are your big sisters, Lou and Amy. And this is Scott. Say hello."

"Aloo," Lily managed, grinning widely.

"She's adorable," Lou enthused.

"Come on, Lily," Helena took Lily out of Tim's arms. "We'll unload the bags while you have a cuddle with your big sisters."

Before Amy knew what was happening, Helena had passed Lily to her. She cradled the baby in her arms and gazed down into her large brown eyes. "Hello," Amy murmured awkwardly, not knowing what else to say.

To her discomfort, Lily started to look anxious. She continued to stare at Amy but her lips turned down at the corners and her eyes filled with tears.

Oh no, Amy thought, *please don't cry*. But Lily began to sob and even though Amy jiggled her, she didn't stop. If anything, her cries grew louder.

"Here," said Lou, gently lifting Lily out of Amy's arms. She held the baby upright so she could look over her shoulder and gently hushed her. Within moments Lily's cries had subsided.

"You're a natural," Helena congratulated Lou.

Everyone laughed, but Amy felt her cheeks flush. She was relieved that Lou had taken the baby and stopped her crying, but she still felt awful that Lily had screamed with her. And, though she tried to push it away, she couldn't help but feel a little resentful towards Helena for thrusting Lily on her like that.

Almost as if she had guessed Amy's thoughts, Helena turned to her and smiled brightly. "How did the flight go?" she asked, but before Amy could answer she continued. "You must be tired. I've got your bedroom ready. It's next to Lou's. All of our guest bedrooms are in the loft. We had it converted last year. I've laid out some clean towels for you and there's shower gel in your bathroom. Do you want to go up now or would you rather eat first? I wasn't sure what you liked, so I—"

"I think what Amy would really like is to go and see the horses," Tim interrupted with a smile.

Amy couldn't help noticing Helena's nervous chatter, and she wondered why her stepmother was trying so hard.

"Of course," Helena agreed with a quick half-smile. "I should have guessed — like father, like daughter." She gave a little laugh before turning to Lou and Scott. "Would you like something to eat or drink?" she asked. "I've got cold drinks waiting for you on the veranda, along with some snacks."

"A cold drink sounds great," Scott replied cheerfully, rolling up the sleeves of his shirt and stooping to pick up some of the bags.

Tim had obviously noticed the longing look Amy had cast at the stable block because he turned to Scott. "Leave the bags, I'll bring them in later," he said. "You go into the house with Helena and Lou, and relax. You must be exhausted after all those hours flying. I'll just give Amy a quick tour of the yard and introduce her to the horses."

Amy turned towards the stables eagerly before suddenly stopping and clasping her hand to her head. "I promised to call and let Grandpa know we'd arrived safely," she said.

"I'll do that," Lou offered.

"Thanks, Lou. Can you pass on my love and ask him to tell Ty that I'll call him soon?"

"Sure," Lou replied, and Amy turned and followed Tim across the gravel drive to the modern stable block.

"How's Ty getting on now that he's home from hospital?" Tim asked as they crunched across the small stones.

"He's still not a hundred per cent," Amy told him. "I just hope he doesn't push himself too hard while I'm away."

"No doubt you made it very clear to him exactly what he should and shouldn't do?" Tim said, sounding amused.

Amy bit her lip but couldn't help grinning. "Just a little," she admitted.

As they drew closer to the yard, Amy looked from side to side, keen to see every small detail.

"Most of the horses are either out being worked or in the paddocks," her father explained. "Sam is fixing some fences in the top fields.. One of my stablehands, Alex, is travelling back from a three-day event with Pat and two of the horses that are just about ready to be sold on."

Amy nodded. Her father's yard seemed to be the well-run, professional establishment she'd been expecting.

As they crossed the yard, Tim strode ahead to run his hands over the shining palomino coat of a large gelding that was being groomed. "This is Finn. He's been with us for about six months now, so he's about halfway through his training," he told Amy. "Caroline's looking after him."

The pretty, auburn-haired stable girl paused in her grooming to grin at Amy, who warmed to her instantly. "Call me Caro; Caroline's too much of a mouthful," she said in a broad Australian accent.

"OK, Caro," Amy said with a smile. "I bet Finn's great to ride," she went on, patting the horse's shoulder.

"You bet your life he is!" Caro enthused. "He's got three fantastic paces, and his lateral work is a dream."

Amy smiled at Caro, knowing immediately that they would get on well during her stay. She was just about to ask more questions about Finn when a clatter of hooves sounded behind her. Amy turned to see a girl of about her own age, leading a bay horse that must have been at least seventeen hands high.

"That's Caspian. He's a Danish Warmblood imported from Holland. He's been with us a month and he's making Emma earn every penny of her money!" Tim declared.

"I thought you brought your horses in from England?" Amy queried.

"That's how the business started," Tim agreed, "but we've

begun importing from various European countries, as well as the States."

Amy only half-heard her father. Her attention was drawn to Caspian who had suddenly stopped and was refusing to be led any further. His coat was beginning to shine with a slight sweat.

"Walk on, Caspian!" Emma's voice rang sharply across the yard. She shot a rueful glance at them as she tried to calm Caspian. Her ponytail was coming undone and she looked flushed and anxious.

The more Caspian danced about, the more likely he was to step on Emma's feet, Amy thought. She watched thoughtfully as Emma stood at Caspian's shoulder, attempting to soothe him and walk him on at the same time. Amy frowned; it was unusual for a horse to act this way out of sheer naughtiness. She noticed that Caspian's ears were pricked forward and his nostrils were flaring widely. Following the animal's gaze, Amy saw that the last stable in the block had its door open. Sticking halfway out of the door was a wheelbarrow and fork. Somehow, an empty sack of feed was caught on the prongs of the fork, flapping gently in the breeze. To a highly strung animal like Caspian, the noise and motion were extremely unsettling.

Instinctively, Amy walked across to Caspian and Emma. "Hi," she said to Emma. "I think I know what's worrying him. Do you mind if I try to walk him past?"

Emma hesitated for a moment and then handed Amy the leading rope. "Be careful, though. If you stand in front of him like that, you might get trampled," she pointed out.

Amy had to admit that it was nerve-wracking standing in

front of such a large, prancing animal instead of safely at his shoulder, but she knew that if she took on the role of a lead horse, Caspian might just calm down enough to follow her.

Presenting her back to Caspian, Amy began to walk ahead of him, applying a firm but gentle pressure to the lead rope. "C'mon boy," she encouraged without turning around.

Caspian snorted loudly but Amy ignored him and kept going, talking soothingly and pulling the rein gently. She felt it slacken – Caspian was following her! As they drew level with the open stable door, Caspian blew air heavily out of his nostrils and skittered sideways, but Amy carried on walking calmly until they were past. Then she turned to the horse and gently stroked his neck. In return, Caspian stood quietly, even though Amy could still feel the tension in his muscles.

Emma had followed them and without a word she now took the rope back from Amy.

"I think he was just scared," Amy said.

"Thanks," Emma replied, not looking at Amy but concentrating instead on stroking Caspian's neck. Tim and Caro joined them.

"Wow, that was great. How did you get him to follow you like that?" Tim asked.

Caro raised her eyebrows "Yeah, let us in on your secret."

Amy smiled, appreciating her interest. "When a horse is scared he often just needs a bit of reassurance. In the wild he would follow the alpha horse past a scary object, so I just took the lead and hoped his natural instincts would take over and make him follow me," she explained.

"Well, it worked," her father said happily.

"Sure did," Emma agreed. She clicked with her tongue and led the bay gelding away.

Amy watched them go and couldn't help feeling that somehow she had done the wrong thing. But before she had time to try and work out why that was, Tim steered her away from Caro and into the tack room at the end of the stable block.

Unlike Heartland's tack room, which was always cluttered, Tim's tack room was large and airy, with saddles lining three walls and bridles hanging neatly on hooks underneath. The room had the familiar smell of saddle soap and Amy noticed that on a table at the back were well-stocked grooming kits.

"This is great!" she exclaimed, turning her attention to the one wall that didn't have tack on it. Row upon row of blue, red and yellow ribbons lined it, alongside shelves of silver cups and plaques. But what really drew Amy's gaze were the pictures.

"Pegasus!" she breathed, walking up to take a closer look. It had been on Pegasus that Tim had suffered the accident that had ended his show-jumping days. Amy's mom had taken the injured horse with them to Virginia and nursed him back to full health using alternative remedies.

There was one particular picture that made Amy's stomach churn with emotion. It showed Tim and Marion standing either side of Pegasus who had his ears pricked forward. On his back was a young girl who Amy immediately recognized as Lou. They all looked so happy that it made the back of Amy's throat ache and her eyes began to sting with tears. She turned to her father and a look of understanding passed between them.

"Come on," said Tim softly. "We have two other residents that I want to introduce you to now."

Amy was very curious about the horses that she was going to meet. Tim led her round the side of the stable block to the second row of loose boxes. He slid back the bolt on the first door and Amy stepped inside. She gasped with pleasure at the beautiful horse that stood looking at her. "What's his name?" she asked, without taking her eyes off the dappled-grey gelding. His long silver mane and tail gave him striking looks.

"Spirit," Tim answered. "And he's yours for the time that you're here," he added.

"Really?" Amy couldn't disguise her delight as she ran her eyes over his sloping shoulder and took in the kind expression in his large, dark eyes. Amy knew instinctively that he was a very special horse.

"I do have a slight hidden agenda," her father admitted.

"How slight?" Amy demanded, pretending to be stern.

"I was hoping you would put in some work on him," Tim replied seriously. "I bought him just over a year ago. Helena fell in love with him so I decided to let her handle him."

"I didn't realize that Helena was so interested in horses," Amy said in surprise.

Tim nodded. "It's how I met her. She'd been staying with a friend in England. The day before her friend was going to ride in a competition, she broke a bone in her wrist. Helena has always ridden and so she took her friend's place. She came third in the dressage, one place below the sire of a youngster I was thinking of buying. I had gone to the event to watch the sire perform before I agreed a sale – and instead found myself asking Helena out for a drink." He gave a small laugh and ran his hand through his curly hair.

"We've had no problem with Spirit until recently," Tim went on. "He developed into an amazing event horse and we could all see that he had the potential to make it to the very top. But then I sent him out to a few shows with different riders, and his performance just wasn't anywhere near what we had expected. It was as if he had lost all enthusiasm for what he was doing. It didn't take me long to work out that he only shines when Helena is riding him. They have this amazing bond between them that, unfortunately, we have to break if we're going to be able to sell him on. Helena has stopped riding Spirit over the past couple of weeks, and I was hoping that you would spend some time with him each day that you're here." He turned to face Amy and winked. "That is, unless you've come here to have a holiday from riding?"

"A vacation without riding? Never!" Amy laughed and walked over to Spirit who had been watching them with interest. She bent down to blow into his nostrils, greeting the horse as another horse would. He blew back heavily, accepting her at once.

"He's lovely, Dad," she said happily.

"That's sorted then. I know you're going to love riding him. He's got fantastic elevated paces," her father told her, leading the way out of the box. "Now, let me introduce you to my second project."

A coal black head was looking over the door of the adjoining box. "This," Tim told Amy, "is Mistral."

Amy didn't think she had ever seen such a stunning horse. "She's an Andalusian, right?" she asked, thinking of the famous Spanish horses. She'd never seen a black one before.

"She's part-Andalusian. Actually, she's a thoroughbred cross," Tim answered as Mistral snaked her head back into the box. "The breed is becoming quite popular in Australia because they're very fast and they can turn on a dollar. In Spain they're used for bull fighting, so it's not surprising they're agile – think of the twists and turns that they'd have to perform in a bullring. There are studs in quite a few states now over here and they compete in dressage, show-jumping, and cross-country events."

"Where did she go?" Amy asked, surprised to see that Mistral had retreated. It was not a reaction she usually got from a horse.

"Well, that's the strange thing about her," Tim said, joining Amy at the door of the box. Mistral was standing in a tucked-up position inside, as far away from them as possible. Her strong, proud neck hung low. "She's something of a mystery," Tim went on. "She just doesn't seem to like human company at all. Whenever we try and work with her, she breaks into a heavy sweat and gets so distressed we have to stop. I imported her six weeks ago from Spain. By now she should be starting to work on basic schooling, but we can't even lunge her without causing her stress. I'm afraid I can only give her a few more weeks before I have to cut my losses and sell her on – which would be a real waste of potential. Do you think you can do anything with her?"

"I'll do what I can," Amy promised. Her mind automatically began to race through the methods she would try with Mistral and Spirit. She was proud that her father had so much confidence in her skills, but most of all, she couldn't wait to spend time with both horses, getting to know them and helping them through their difficulties. Her heart soared as she considered the month ahead. It looked as if staying with her father was going to be even more exciting than she had dreamed!

Chapter Four

Amy leaned out of the window and gave a contented sigh. From her room she had views over the fields that stretched away from the ranch. Two chestnut horses in the closest field were chasing one another playfully. Amy smiled as they cantered in circles, their tails held high.

"Are you ready?" Lou asked, coming into the room. "Dad and Helena have organized a welcome party for us so we can meet everyone here."

"Sounds great," Amy said, turning round and noticing that her sister had changed into a pair of beige trousers and matching top.

"I've just been helping Helena put Lily to bed," Lou told her. "She's so sweet. She grabbed hold of my finger and wouldn't let go."

Amy tried not to think of Lily's initial reaction to her. She slipped on a jacket and followed Lou downstairs and out on to the back patio.

Outside, the patio was crowded with people standing in small groups, illuminated by pretty Chinese lanterns strung overhead. Amy and Lou were introduced to all the people who helped in their father's business. Amy smiled and answered their questions about Heartland enthusiastically, while trying to make a mental note of everyone's name.

"This is terrific," a tall, slim boy with red hair remarked. He was looking hungrily at the bowls of chips, chicken, tasty sausages, relish, boiled eggs and steaming corn on the cob, which were spread over a long trestle table. "I usually go home to beans on toast," he added and grinned.

Amy laughed as he grabbed a plate.

Caro came over to join them. "How did you get on at your event, Alex?" she asked.

Alex's blue eyes crinkled at the corners. "Great, thanks. We placed first – as you'd expect!" he declared.

"Show-off," Caro teased, rolling her eyes towards Amy.

"Just because you only come home with yellow ribbons there's no need to take your insecurities out on me," Alex replied, shaking his head in mock disapproval.

Emma, who was standing a little way off, overheard this last comment and laughed. "At least we know there's more to competitions than just the prizes," she retorted.

Alex pretended to look shocked. "Rubbish! It's a good thing Tim's got me to rely on."

Tim turned from the barbecue and brandished his spatula. "Now then, you guys," he said, "do you think you can take a break from squabbling long enough to eat?"

"You bet!" Alex grinned, holding out his plate.

Tim began to pile the plates up with burgers and sausages. When he reached a large, balding man who was sitting a little way from the group, he paused. "Have you got an hour free to drive into town with me tomorrow, Sam?" Amy heard him ask.

"Shouldn't be a problem, Tim," his manager replied between mouthfuls of potato salad.

Caro unfolded two chairs for herself and Amy, close to the warmth of the barbecue. "Sam never says much. He only talks when he has to," she commented softly. "Although he sometimes asks Alex why he insists on talking so much when he has so little worth saying!"

Amy laughed and glanced at Alex. He was the type of person you couldn't help liking. He was talking animatedly now to a man she hadn't been introduced to. The man was in his thirties with black curly hair and bright blue eyes.

"That's Pat," Caro told her, following her gaze.

Just then, Helena made her way over to them. "Did you get to meet Spirit and Mistral?" she asked, as she dragged a chair over and sat down next to Amy.

Amy nodded in reply.

"What did you think of them?" Helena asked curiously.

"They're both lovely-looking horses," Amy replied enthusiastically. "And I've never worked with a horse that is part-Andalusian before. I can't wait to see Mistral moving – I bet she's got fantastic paces! Spirit is beautiful, too. I can tell just by looking at him that he's got a wonderful personality."

Helena nodded and smiled. "I expect Tim told you that Spirit was my horse?"

"Yes, he said that you turned him into an amazing eventer," Amy told her.

"Really?" Helena laughed and raised an eyebrow at Tim. "He's never said that to me. He usually complains that I spoil him."

Everyone laughed and Amy felt the warmth between Tim and Helena. She smiled, but inside she was struggling with emotion. She couldn't remember her mom and dad being together. Tim had met and married Helena a few years ago. Amy knew it wasn't fair that she should find it difficult being with Tim and his new wife, but a small part of her still wanted him just for herself and Lou.

As Amy wrestled with her feelings, she noticed that Helena had turned to Scott and was asking him about his conference. That left Amy free to wander across and ask Emma how Caspian had gone for her that afternoon.

"Fine," Emma replied shortly, immediately turning to Alex and beginning a discussion about the best way to jump a course she had set up that afternoon.

Amy felt hurt by the fact that Emma clearly didn't want to start a conversation with her. She wondered why, but she tried not to dwell on it – after all, everyone else had been friendly and welcoming. And Amy couldn't wait to take Spirit out for a ride!

Later that evening, Amy called Ty. She felt a rush of homesickness the moment she heard the familiar sound of his voice.

"How's it going?" he asked warmly.

"OK," she replied, and immediately launched into a million questions about Heartland. "How are you and Grandpa? Is Marnie managing OK? What about Ben and Red – and how's Dazzle coming along?"

"Hey, slow down!" Ty laughed. "We're all fine. Ben's really

pleased with Red's jumping and Dazzle is getting better with every session. He seems to be really enjoying the work now. Your Grandpa's doing just fine with all the instructions Lou left for him, and Marnie's getting on well with Candy."

"And the rest of the horses?" Amy asked anxiously.

"Amy!" Ty said firmly. "You've got to stop worrying about how things are here. You're supposed to be enjoying yourself with your new family. Now, tell me what's happened since you arrived."

Amy quickly filled him in on everyone she had met, and then went on to talk about the horses – especially Spirit and Mistral. Ty listened attentively. "They sound great. Just don't spend so much time working with the horses that you miss out on time with Tim, Helena and Lily," he reminded her.

Amy sighed. She knew it was a good point, she just found the horses so much easier to relate to. "I miss you," she said quietly.

I miss you, too," Ty replied.

"And I'll email soon," Amy promised, before saying goodbye and hanging up. Suddenly she felt much happier.

Amy woke the next morning to find she had slept for a full twelve hours. She couldn't remember the last time she had slept round the clock. The long journey to Australia had obviously worn her out. She quickly pulled on some clothes and hurried downstairs just in time to say goodbye to Scott as he left for his conference.

Scott and Tim were stowing his bags in the truck with Lou standing by.

"Phew," said Scott, pushing his hair off his forehead. His eyes suddenly lighted on Amy. "I thought you were never going to wake up!" he said, and grinned before turning to hug Lou goodbye.

Tim was holding the door open for him. "Thanks for everything," said Scott as he shook Tim's hand.

"No problem," Tim replied, "I'll be interested in hearing about it when you get back."

Pat started the engine and, as the truck rolled away, Amy noticed a wistful look in Lou's eyes. "He'll be back soon," she said and squeezed her sister's arm.

"I know," Lou made an effort to look brighter. "And I'm really looking forward to today. Helena and I are taking Lily into town and then to a neighbour's ranch. Are you going to come?"

Amy thought about it for a moment, but she was longing to get down to the yard and see the horses. She shook her head. "I'd love to, but…" she began.

"I know, I know," Lou laughed. "You want to see Spirit and Mistral."

Amy smiled. "Maybe we can ride out together this afternoon?" she suggested.

"I think we're going to be gone for most of the day. I'm sure we'll get a chance to ride out soon, though," Lou promised.

There was the sound of footsteps crunching on the gravel as Helena joined them. "How about a nice big breakfast to set you up for the day?" she smiled. "I've done hash browns, eggs and bacon."

They all walked back inside. Lou and Helena talked happily about their schedule for the day and Amy's thoughts drifted away to her own plans for Spirit and Mistral.

Amy decided to work with Mistral first. When she went into the loose box with a lead rope in her hand, the big black horse snorted nervously and backed into the far corner. Amy bit her lower lip as she gazed at the mare. Her eyes were large, bright and placed widely apart, which told Amy that Mistral had a kind temperament. It didn't make sense that she was so nervous with people. Tim had assured Amy that the horse had never been abused and that Mistral's only previous owner had a good reputation.

Amy chatted reassuringly to Mistral as she clipped on the rope and led her out to the training arenas behind the ranch. Emma was in the jumping ring and Amy paused to watch her ride a showy chestnut over a course of eight jumps. They moved together in perfect symmetry and Amy realized that Emma was a first-class rider, giving exactly the right balance of encouragement and guidance to the young horse.

Mistral began to grow a little restless and Amy led her on into the centre of the all-weather arena before halting again. She knew that joining-up with Mistral was the best way to gain her trust so that the healing process could begin. She unclipped the lead rope and Mistral instantly moved away from her. It was clear that the mare didn't want to share her personal space.

Amy flicked the end of the rope out and Mistral swung away to the outside of the arena. Patches of sweat were already forming on her flanks. Amy flicked the rope again and Mistral began to canter around. After a while Amy frowned, concerned, for Mistral was showing all the signs of misery. Amy would have expected the mare to have begun to settle and relax by this stage, but her tail was clamped tightly down, her eyes were wide with tension and her nostrils were flaring. Amy persevered, hoping that soon the mare would begin to show signs of wanting to join her in the centre of the ring. But it was easy to see how tired Mistral was getting. Her sides were visibly moving in and out and she was cantering more and more slowly.

"She's really not that fit, you know," Emma said, breaking Amy's concentration.

Amy glanced across to the entrance of the arena where Emma stood watching. Mistral took advantage of Amy's lapse in concentration to halt in the far corner. Amy sighed. She knew it would be best now to cut her losses and call an end to the session. Mistral was too tired to begin all over again. As she walked over to collect Mistral, Amy noticed Emma give her a slightly disapproving look before riding away.

Amy stuck her chin out mutinously at Emma's retreating figure. "She doesn't know what I was trying to do, does she?" Amy murmured to the mare as she led her back to the yard. "The problem is," she added sadly, "neither do you."

After Amy had seen to Mistral she carried Spirit's tack to his box. The horse looked at her with interest and Amy couldn't help breathing a sigh of relief that he seemed pleased at the prospect of being ridden.

She warmed him up and then began to ride some basic schooling movements. Spirit obeyed her perfectly, but that's all it was, obedience – a well-trained horse carrying out her commands. Everything she did with Spirit felt flat; he simply wasn't allowing her into a partnership with him.

She spoke encouragingly and noticed that his ear barely flickered back. "Let's see how you jump," she told him and set him at a practice bar in the middle of the ring. But there was no surge of enthusiasm, as Amy would usually expect. If Spirit had been human, he would have yawned as he popped over the jump, rattling the top bar with his hooves.

Tim was waiting for her when she got back into the yard. "How did it go?" he asked as he opened the loose-box door.

"Hmmm," Amy replied. "You were right about his lack of enthusiasm." She slipped off Spirit and led him into his box.

"Give it some time," Tim advised.

Amy nodded. "If I write you out a list, is there a health shop in town where you could collect some herbs and remedies for me?" she queried.

"I should think so," Tim replied. "Leave it with me."

Amy helped herself to some sandwiches Helena had thoughtfully left out for her lunch. Then she decided to go back down into the yard and see if there was anything she could do.

Emma was outside the stable block with Caspian, picking out his hooves. Amy decided to try and make an effort. "Hi," she called. "Do you want a hand?"

"I can manage, thanks," Emma said shortly. Before Amy could reply, Emma went on. "Hadn't you better check on your own horses instead of worrying about mine? Mistral was in such a state this morning, she probably needs a second rubdown."

Amy felt her cheeks burn. "Just what is your problem?" she asked indignantly, but Emma ignored her, tugged Caspian's slip tie undone, and led him away to the paddocks.

As Amy stood staring at Emma's back, she heard a movement behind her.

"Alex and I were just about to ride out," Caro said and smiled. "If you fancy coming along, you could ride Jinx for me. You'd be doing me a favour – it will save me exercising him later, and it'll be good to start getting him used to different riders."

Amy couldn't tell if Caro had overheard her exchange with Emma, but she felt a rush of relief at her friendliness. "That sounds great," she said warmly.

Within ten minutes the three of them were clattering out of the yard. Alex was riding a big black gelding called Zeus. "He's already got a buyer lined up," Alex said, patting his neck.

"He's in great shape," Amy remarked. Zeus didn't have a spare ounce of fat on him and was clearly at the peak of fitness.

"Why, thanks, sport. Now then, Miss F, are you up to tackling our cross-country course or do you want something a little more sedate?" Alex asked in a deliberately exaggerated Australian accent.

Amy laughed and felt a surge of excitement at the thought of taking Jinx over some jumps. It was just what she needed after her difficult morning. "Let's go for it," she said eagerly.

"The course starts just on the other side of those trees to your right," Caro said, pointing. "Jinx has got a great bold jump but he can be a bit of a baby on the approach, so he needs to feel that you're with him every step of the way."

Amy nodded and patted Jinx's golden neck reassuringly before shortening her stirrup leathers.

As they rode through an opening in the trees, Amy saw that a small course had been made stretching over two fields and disappearing into the distance.

"There's no jump over one metre, OK?" asked Alex.

Amy nodded.

"If you let me get one jump in front of you, then follow the line that I take, you'll be fine," Alex assured her.

They all checked their girths and began to warm the horses up. When Alex left them to tackle the first jump – which was a huge felled tree trunk – Jinx snorted and plunged. Amy settled him by asking him, gently but firmly, to accept the bit before sending him forward. Jinx flew over the tree with a powerful surge and Amy felt a rush of adrenaline. She had to remind herself to hold Jinx at a steady canter – instead of letting him gallop as they would both have liked. "Steady now, you may know you're way around, but I don't," she murmured as a spread loomed in front of them.

The rest of the course passed by in a blur and Jinx didn't falter once. Under Amy's guidance he cleared each jump with an enthusiasm that had her breathless by the time she drew up next to Alex. "That was incredible!" she exclaimed delightedly.

"You both look as if you could go round again," Alex laughed as Caro cantered up.

"Jinx looked great with you," Caro told Amy.

"He was fantastic," Amy admitted as they turned for home. They went at a slow pace to give the horses the opportunity to cool down.

"Do you have a course back at home?" Alex asked.

Amy smiled, thinking of the basic facilities they had at Heartland. "Everything we have at home is geared towards rehabilitating the horses that come to us. We have some jumps in one of the rings, but mostly we work on the flat," she explained.

"Tim said that you do a lot of alternative stuff," Caro remarked.

"Sounds a bit of a waste of time to me," Alex commented. "No offence," he added hurriedly as Caro frowned at him.

"It's OK. Ben, one of our stablehands, thought that when he first joined us," Amy smiled. "He's come round to our way of thinking now that he's seen the results."

"Your dad certainly thinks it's got a lot going for it," Alex admitted. "He talks a lot about the work that you do."

Amy felt a rush of warmth. "Does he?" She couldn't help feeling pleased. Her dad's opinion meant a lot to her.

"Yep, he reckons you're building up quite a reputation for yourself in Virginia."

"It's not just me," said Amy quickly. "I couldn't do it without Ty and Ben and Lou and Grandpa – we're a team."

"It's the same here," Caro said, nodding her head. "I think the main reason we get such good results with the horses is because we work so well together."

Amy went quiet as she thought about Caro's words. She knew that everyone at Heartland had wanted her to come out to her father's ranch, but she still felt a little guilty.

"Are you OK?" Caro asked and glanced at Amy as they rode into the yard.

Amy saw concern written across Caro's face and thought again how nice she was. "I'm just feeling a little bad that I've left everyone else to carry on with the work at home while I'm here," she admitted.

"I understand that. If I'm away from here, even for a long weekend, I start itching to come back. After all, no one can look after my horses as well as I can!" Caro joked, but then a serious expression came into her eyes. "You shouldn't feel bad. What you do at Heartland is great, but you've got other important things in your life, too – like family."

Amy nodded, she knew that what Caro was saying made sense, but she had given Heartland one hundred per cent since her mom's death. Now she found it difficult to do anything else.

After showering and changing, Amy wandered down to the kitchen to find Lou playing with Lily in her highchair. Helena was busy making a Bolognese and Amy volunteered to set the table.

"Actually, I've already set it out on the veranda tonight. But it would be great if you could feed Lily her dinner for me – it's in the bowl on the table," Helena answered.

Amy looked at the green plastic bowl and then at Lily who was staring at her. She picked up the bowl. "Sure, no problem," she replied, feeling rather apprehensive as she sat down next to Lily.

"How did your day go?" Lou asked, getting up and filling a pan with boiling water.

"Um, OK," said Amy distractedly as she tried to persuade Lily to eat. It was some kind of yellow gloop which looked disgusting – especially as it oozed back out of Lily's mouth.

"Here," Helena said, smiling and passing her a napkin.

Amy tried not to pull a face as she wiped the substance away from Lily's mouth. Unfortunately, the more she wiped, the more of Lily's face it seemed to cover. Lily pushed at the napkin, getting gloop all over her hands, too.

"How did your sessions go with the horses?" Helena asked.

"Not great, but then they rarely do in the early stages," Amy responded. For some reason she felt a little defensive, but neither Lou nor Helena seemed to notice.

"I always found that Spirit responded well when I told him what we were going to do before giving him the actual aids to do it," Helena commented. "That way it felt as if we were in on it together, rather than me just making him obey."

Amy felt a stirring of resentment at Helena's advice. A slight frown creased her forehead. She didn't know what was wrong; normally she appreciated other people's input on the horses she was working with. It was probably jetlag, she decided as she returned her attention to Lily.

Amy tried to make Lily more interested in her meal by talking to her. "Mmm, Lily, look, yummy food just for you," she offered. But Lily pressed her lips into a thin line and refused to eat any more.

"I'm sorry," Amy said, "she just doesn't want it."

"Here, you finish the spaghetti," Lou said, taking over. She pretended that the spoon of food was an aeroplane and zoomed it towards Lily's mouth. Lily giggled and opened her mouth wide.

As Lou and Helena chatted easily, Amy concentrated on stirring the spaghetti. *What am I doing wrong with Lily?* she thought, glancing at the baby who was now smiling happily up at Lou. Amy sighed inwardly and tried not to listen to the voice in her head which whispered that maybe she just didn't belong in her dad's new family.

Chapter Five

After a couple of days at her father's ranch, Amy managed to find time to send some emails home. She leaned back in her chair and read over the last few lines of her message to Soraya. *I think that Spirit might end up being as difficult to reach as Mistral. I just hope that I can make a difference before it's time to leave.*

Just as she was about to add another line she heard her sister's bedroom door open. Amy left the computer and looked out into the hallway.

"Morning," Lou said.

"Hi," Amy replied. "I'm just finishing an email and then, after breakfast, I'm going to ride Spirit and Mistral. Do you want to come down and meet them?"

"I'd love to," Lou agreed eagerly. Then she clapped her hand to her head. "Oh, I forgot! I'm really sorry, I've already arranged to go out walking with Helena this morning. We're going to put Lily in her baby carrier and hike up to one of the local beauty spots. Why don't you join us?"

"I would," said Amy regretfully, "but I've planned to concentrate on Spirit and Mistral this morning. I really need to join-up with Mistral — we didn't have a very successful session yesterday."

Lou looked sympathetic.

"I'll put aside some time for Lily soon," Amy promised. "I'd like to get to know her better."

"I was beginning to think she needed to grow a mane and tail to get your attention," Lou sighed.

Amy felt a little guilty. Then she caught sight of the mischievous twinkle in her sister's eyes and they both burst into laughter.

"You could have made a bit more of an effort," Amy muttered as she led Spirit back into his loose box. Once again he had behaved impeccably, but with absolutely no enthusiasm for any of the work Amy had asked him to do. He had tipped the poles on most of the jumps, and his flatwork had lacked any zeal. "You've got to try harder," she told him sternly.

Spirit rubbed his head against her arm where he was itching under his bridle.

"OK, OK," she sighed. "I get the message."

When Amy let herself into Mistral's box, the mare regarded her suspiciously but, for the first time, didn't back away from her. Amy had spent ages grooming her before breakfast and Mistral's coal black coat gleamed. The mare had appeared to relax towards the end of the grooming session and Amy wanted to try and recapture that mood before taking her out to the school. She tipped a little lavender oil into her hands and began to massage it into Mistral's coat, hoping the oil's relaxing qualities would help.

After five minutes, Amy slipped Mistral's headcollar on. Immediately the mare grew tense. "Easy," Amy soothed and began to massage Mistral's neck gently, in small, T-touch circles until she felt the muscles relax. "OK, girl, walk on," Amy said and led her from the box.

Once in the middle of the schooling ring, Amy released Mistral and tapped her lightly on the hindquarters to send her away to the edge of the ring. The black horse broke into a powerful trot and Amy took up an aggressive stance to encourage her into a canter. Mistral completed five circuits before Amy sent her around in the opposite direction. It took a while, but eventually Mistral began to show signs of wanting to join Amy in the centre of the ring. Amy turned her body sideways to the horse and lowered her eyes. She needed Mistral to sense that she was not a threat to her. She could hear Mistral slow her pace until she came to a halt. Then came the sound that Amy was waiting for; the soft, sweet thud of hooves on sand as Mistral made her way over to Amy.

"Good girl," Amy whispered as she moved away and Mistral followed. Amy wanted to make a fuss of her, but knew that Mistral would flinch away from the attention, so she quietly clipped the lead rein back on to the mare's headcollar and headed back to the yard. As she left the school, she noticed Emma watching her. Amy didn't know how long she had been there but, when she raised her hand in a friendly wave, Emma quickly turned away. Amy sighed. She was beginning to wonder if she and Emma would ever get on.

After turning Spirit and Mistral out in the paddocks, Amy wandered back up to the ranch house. Lou was pushing Lily gently on a special swing that Tim had made for her out of a car tyre. He had fashioned a head, tail, and saddle for the tyre to make a swaying horse and Lily was gurgling with laughter at every push.

Lou saw Amy and paused. "How did it go with the horses?" she asked.

Before Amy could tell her sister about her progress with Mistral, Lily called out. "Again, Oow, again."

"Oow?" Amy asked, raising an eyebrow.

"It's what she calls me," Lou said shyly. "She started saying it this morning."

The screen door banged and Helena appeared on the veranda carrying bowls of salad. "Hi," she said and smiled. "Tim's just washing up inside, we'll have lunch as soon as he's ready."

"I'd better wash, too," said Amy. "I won't be long."

When she came back, Tim was sitting at the table drinking a glass of water. It was the first time he had joined them for lunch. Amy hadn't realized just how busy he would be. She thought of how hard she worked at Heartland and knew it must be the same for her father here. But she was determined to make more of an effort to spend time with him.

"Hi," Tim said, looking up. "How did you get on today?"

"Good, thanks," replied Amy enthusiastically. She told him about Mistral.

Tim listened intently. "Well done," he said warmly when Amy had finished.

"It's only the first small step," Amy added quickly.

"But at least it's in the right direction," Helena put in. She glanced up at Amy and Tim. "How do the two of you feel about a ride out this afternoon? Lou offered to babysit Lily, so I thought we could ride down to Fiddler's Creek."

"That sounds like a great idea. I've got a bit of free time this afternoon," Tim agreed enthusiastically. He turned to Lou, "Are you sure you don't mind? You haven't ridden at all yet."

"It's fine," Lou assured him. "I'm going to do some finger-painting with Lily."

Amy glanced at her sister and was struck by how happy and relaxed she looked. Her blue eyes shone brightly and already her skin had a slight glow from the warm Australian sun. "Thanks, Lou," she said warmly. "Maybe we can ride out together tomorrow?"

"That sounds great," Lou replied. She lifted Lily out of her high chair. "Let's go find your apron," she said, breaking into a wide smile as Lily reached to her.

Amy suddenly remembered that she had promised Lou she would spend some time getting to know Lily better. *I'll try and do something with her tomorrow*, she thought.

Amy was tightening Spirit's girth when Tim and Helena led their horses round from the other side of the stable block. Spirit stiffened as he caught sight of Helena. He let out a long nicker and strained to reach her.

Amy glanced up to see a frustrated look on Helena's face as she smoothed Spirit's nose and turned away. It was clear that she would have loved to pay more attention to Spirit. Amy suddenly felt a stab of sympathy for Helena. She knew what it felt like to develop a deep bond with a horse – and knew how awful it must be for Helena to have to keep her distance.

"That's a beautiful horse," Amy said to Helena, trying to lighten the mood.

"Thank you," Helena smiled, stroking the satiny neck of the small horse. "Her name's Lace. She's an Arabian."

"Ready?" Tim interrupted as the large gelding he was riding began to prance on the spot.

Amy swung herself lightly into the saddle and shortened her reins. "Ready," she told him.

It took just under an hour to reach the creek. As the horses lowered their heads to drink from the water, Helena complimented Amy on her riding. "Spirit goes very well for you," she said.

"But not in the ring," Amy replied, and grimaced, making Helena laugh.

"I have a feeling you're going to break through with him – just keep trying," encouraged Helena with a smile.

"Thanks," Amy said and, looking into Helena's sincere brown eyes, she felt, for the first time, a slight warming towards her.

They made their way along the winding, tree-lined track, back towards the ranch, and Amy thought how nice it would be if she could get along with Helena in the same way that Lou did. *Why is it that Lou finds it so easy to get on with Helena and I don't?* Amy asked herself as she leaned forward and flipped Lace's mane so that it was all lying on the same side of her neck. Then she gave a small sigh. All she really knew was that the only time she felt truly comfortable on her father's ranch was when she was working with Spirit and Mistral.

After they had ridden back to the ranch and seen to the horses, Helena suggested cold drinks on the veranda. As they approached the house, Amy saw Lou and Lily waving to them. Tim's face broke into a big smile as he held out his arms to Lily.

"How's my beautiful girl?" he asked, lifting her up on to his shoulders.

Lily squealed with laughter and held out her hands to Helena.

Helena rescued her and stood her on the ground. "Why don't you sit on Amy's lap while Mummy gets some drinks?" she suggested.

Amy suddenly remembered her promise to spend more time with Lily. She walked across and smiled down at the little girl.

"Do you want me to push you on your swing, Lily?" she asked gently.

Lily stared at Amy solemnly for a moment before raising her arms. Delighted, Amy lifted her on to her swing and began to push. Lily gurgled happily as she swung back and forth and Amy felt surprised at how much she was enjoying being with her little sister.

After a few minutes, the screen door banged and Lou emerged with a tray of glasses.

"Oow, oow," Lily called the moment she saw her. She began to wriggle in the swing seat. Amy hurriedly stopped pushing and lifted Lily up. But before she had a chance to do anything, Lily squirmed in her arms. "Oow!" she called again.

Lou stepped over and took Lily. "It's just because I've spent a lot of time with her, that's all," she said, obviously trying to make Amy feel better.

Amy nodded but inside she was disappointed. She had just begun to feel like part of the family, and now she felt like an outsider once again.

Once Lily had been put to bed that evening, Tim showed Amy into his den and produced a home video from his library. "This will give you a good idea of just what Spirit's capable of," he explained. "I filmed Helena riding a Preliminary test. Watch it and see what you think."

He clicked on the VCR and snapped off the light so that the room was in darkness. Amy leaned forward to concentrate on the screen.

Although the test was a novice one, from the moment Spirit entered the arena to the moment he departed, there was no doubting his potential for greatness. Amy searched for the right word to describe him, and the one that came to mind was "sparkle". He performed every action with a zest that left other horses looking dull and lifeless by comparison.

She watched the video three times, noting the way Helena and Spirit seemed to know what each other was thinking. The bond between them was obvious.

"Well?" asked Tim when Amy finally switched off the television. "Do you think you can get him back on track?"

"I don't know," Amy admitted honestly. "His performance on tape was awesome." She looked thoughtful. "I think the first stage is to get him to bond with me properly – but not too much, or we might be faced with the same problem again!" She smiled ruefully. "The next step will be to see that Spirit is ridden not only by me. That way, he hasn't got the option of bonding too strongly with just one person." As she spoke she was filled with a new optimism. She felt sure she could overcome Spirit's problems, and suddenly, she couldn't wait to get working with him again.

Amy spent an hour with Mistral the following morning before breakfast, grooming and talking to her. Once the mare was relaxed she led her down to the schooling ring.

Amy noticed her father and Emma walking down to the ringside to watch and she silently willed Mistral to co-operate as she snapped the lunging line on to the mare's halter. Mistral fidgeted nervously.

"It's OK," Amy soothed before sending the horse away from her.

She clicked to Mistral to walk around the ring, but the mare refused to move. The whites of her eyes were showing and her ears were flat against her head. Amy flicked her whip slightly to encourage Mistral forward, but instead the mare ran a few steps backwards and reared up in the air. Amy maintained a steady hold on the lead line, terrified that Mistral might fall over and hurt herself.

As soon as the mare dropped back down to the ground, Amy

walked over to her, talking soothingly the whole time. Mistral was sweating heavily. "It's OK, it's OK," Amy said as she deftly unbuckled the lunging headcollar.

As soon as she was free, Mistral snorted and wheeled away. Amy thought fast. She didn't want to distress the mare any further and yet she couldn't leave the training session on such an unsuccessful note. If she did, she knew that was what Mistral would remember for the next time – and that would seriously impede Amy's progress with her.

Amy knew she had to take control of the situation. Once again she took up her position in the centre of the ring and, using the schooling whip, made Mistral stay out on the track and complete circuits in a controlled trot. She made her change direction twice, all the time reinforcing the fact that she was in charge.

After five minutes, Amy was satisfied that she had salvaged the training session, and she allowed Mistral to halt.

"Well done," Tim said, holding the gate open for her.

Amy had been so engrossed with Mistral that she had forgotten all about Tim and Emma watching.

"I didn't think you'd get her to co-operate after the lunging, but you did exactly the right thing," he went on, running his eyes over the mare.

"Are you sure she hasn't been badly treated, Dad?" Amy asked.

Tim shook his head. "It did cross my mind," he admitted. "But she was sold to me unbacked and from a good yard. I know that there are places that break their horses using harsh methods, but that wouldn't apply to Mistral since the only training she's had so far is to be led in hand."

Emma joined them as they walked back up to the yard.

"I asked Emma to come down with me because I've got a suggestion for you both," Tim began. He glanced at Amy. "How are you managing, handling both Spirit and Mistral?"

Amy wasn't sure what this had to do with her and Emma but she smiled as she replied. "Fine, Dad, I'm used to doing a lot more back home. In fact, I'd love it if there was more for me to do around the yard."

"That's good," said Tim, smiling. "I was hoping that you could spend a little time with Emma and Caspian. Maybe show them a few of the methods you use at Heartland? I'm hoping that Emma can then pass on what she learns to the rest of my staff. I'm really keen to start using some alternative remedies with my horses."

Tim's suggestion was clearly as much of a surprise to Emma as it was to herself, Amy realized, if the horrified expression on Emma's face was anything to go by. Tim was waiting for her answer. "No problem, as long as it's OK with Emma," Amy said cautiously.

Tim looked across at Emma who, now that they had reached the yard, was fiddling with a strand of Mistral's mane. "That would be fine," she answered in a flat voice without looking up. Tim didn't seem to notice that there was anything wrong, but Amy had serious misgivings. *Emma has made it clear*, Amy thought, *that she wants as little to do with me as possible. Now how am I going to overcome that?*

* * *

Helena was in the office when Amy and Tim arrived back at the yard. She came out when she heard them. "Productive session?" she asked Amy.

"Not one of my better ones," Amy replied ruefully.

Helena gave her a sympathetic smile before turning to Tim. "I've just had to reorganize some of the yard schedule," she told him. "You had a phone call earlier to rearrange the delivery time of the new horse. He's not arriving tomorrow morning now, but the day after instead."

Tim frowned briefly. "That's when we're going to be at the auction," he said.

Helena nodded. "It's OK. I've asked Sam to collect the horse instead."

"Thanks," Tim smiled.

Helena pulled the office door shut. "Lou's cooking breakfast today," she told them. "So I hope you're feeling hungry."

Once they were sitting round the table, tucking into bacon, scrambled eggs and sausages, Helena turned to Amy. "Why wasn't it one of your better sessions with Mistral?" she inquired.

"She reacted quite badly when I tried to lunge her," Amy admitted.

"I expect you're used to setbacks, though, from what Tim's told me about your work?" Helena asked with interest.

Amy was about to describe some of the problem horses she had worked with, when Lily spilled her cup of orange juice over herself. Her cries meant Helena was immediately distracted and Amy found herself thinking about her father's suggestion that she should help Emma with Caspian. She tried to work out why Emma should be so unfriendly towards her. Emma was very different when she was with Alex and Caro, so Amy knew it had to be personal.

"What's wrong?" Lou asked, sitting down next to Amy and looking at her with concern.

Amy was suddenly aware of her father's eyes on her as well. "Nothing," she replied quickly. The last thing she wanted to do was create any problems on her father's yard.

Lou didn't look convinced, but she didn't push it. "I thought I'd come and take a look at Spirit and Mistral later this morning – if that's OK?" she suggested

Amy's spirits lifted. "Of course it's OK," she replied happily. She was looking forward to spending some time with her sister.

Amy had tethered Spirit to a ring in the yard and was just leading Mistral out when Lou emerged from Tim's office – a converted loose box at one end of the stable block.

Amy walked Mistral round in a circle, proud of her gleaming black coat and long silky mane, but Lou showed more interest in Spirit. She gave Mistral a vague pat before crossing over to the gelding. "He's beautiful," she enthused. "Helena's told me all about him."

"He's lovely to ride," said Amy. "How about we go out together? You can ride Spirit and I'll ask Dad if I can take one of the other horses."

Spirit blew heavily on Lou's hair and she laughed. "OK. I'd like that," she said.

Amy felt pleased. Lou had only just started riding again. As a child she had loved horses, but her father's show-jumping accident – and then his departure from the family – had affected Lou deeply. She had become fearful around horses and lost all confidence in her own riding ability. Amy hoped that riding Spirit would help Lou regain her confidence and overcome the traumatic effects of her dad's accident.

Tim joined them and Amy immediately asked him if she could take one of the other horses out.

"Sure," he replied. "Take Lace, if you like. I know Helena's not planning to ride today." He looked pleased to hear that Lou was going riding. "I'd love to come with you but I've got mountains of paperwork to get through," he told them regretfully.

"I'll just slip up to the house and get changed. Then we can go," said Lou. As she walked away, Mistral turned her head and watched her go. Amy noticed and felt faintly surprised. She had never seen the mare show the slightest interest in anyone before. She shrugged as she led Mistral back into her box; maybe it had just been a coincidence.

As Amy and Lou rode out from the yard, Lou let out a contented sigh, "This is wonderful," she declared happily, gazing out over the tree-lined fields.

"Shall we ride down to Fiddler's creek?" Amy suggested. "I went there yesterday with Helena and Dad. It's a great ride."

"Sounds fine," said Lou easily. "Do you know, this is probably the best holiday I've ever had? Spending this time with Dad makes me feel that I'm catching up a little on the years I missed with him. And I'm really glad he married Helena – she's so warm and friendly."

Amy was quiet as Lou enthused about their father and his new family. She thought about how Lou had been close to their father until she was twelve years old, while she had only known him for the first few years of her life. The time she was spending at the ranch now was reminding her more and more of just how much she had missed out on.

"What do you think of Lily?" Lou asked, breaking in on Amy's thoughts.

"She's cute," Amy replied, remembering Lily's gurgling laughter when she was pushed on the swing. Thinking of how Lily had wanted to leave the swing and go to Lou made Amy realize that she needed to spend more time with her baby sister. She resolved to make more of an effort during the rest of her stay.

"Are you OK to canter here?" she asked, changing the subject as they turned into a long field that rose up a slight hill. Lou hesitated and Amy sensed her anxiety.

"I promise you'll be fine," Amy told her reassuringly. "Spirit's got an incredibly smooth pace, and your seat is really well balanced!"

Lou looked at Amy questioningly. "Do you really think so?"

Amy thought about what a great natural rider her sister was – and what a shame it was that she'd lost her confidence. "Hey, with our parents, we can't help but be great riders," Amy teased and she was pleased to see Lou smile in response. "Come on, I'll go in front, OK?" Amy said and shortened her reins before nudging Lace into a smooth trot. Once she could see that Lou was posting in a relaxed way on Spirit, she sat deep into her saddle and pushed Lace into a slow, controlled canter. She heard Spirit change his stride behind her and, when she glanced back over her shoulder, she saw Lou riding easily with a big grin on her face.

Amy pulled Lace up at the top of the hill and looked at the view spread out in front of her. She could just make out glimpses between the trees of the snaking line that was Fiddler's creek. The strong sunlight was glinting on the water, turning it into a silver ribbon.

Lou drew Spirit to a halt and patted him. "He's lovely. I can't see why Dad needs you to work on him," she remarked to Amy.

"He does go better on hacks," Amy agreed. "It's in the ring that there's more of a problem. He just lacks any enthusiasm."

"How do you make a horse keen?" Lou queried as they began to ride down towards the creek. "I can see how you could eventually gain a scared horse's confidence, or get a disobedient horse to obey you, but how do you make a well-behaved horse enthusiastic?"

"I'm starting to wonder myself," Amy admitted. "I just hope that by spending lots of time with Spirit I can lessen the bond he's formed with Helena and start getting him to perform well for other riders."

"Well, whatever faults he has in the ring, Helena's done a fantastic job on him," said Lou, stroking Spirit's proud, arched neck. "She must be pretty talented to get an unbacked horse to this standard within a year. Especially considering she had Lily to look after."

"She's done no more than our own mom did when we were little," Amy interrupted. "Only she had the two of us then and her show-jumping career."

"OK!" Lou looked surprised at how defensive Amy sounded. "I wasn't even thinking of comparing Helena to Mom. I was just commenting on the hard work she must have put in on Spirit, on top of everything else she had to do."

Amy chewed her lower lip. She was surprised at her defensive outburst, too. She just couldn't help resenting Lou's clear admiration of Helena, when their own mother had done just as much – and more – when she had been alive.

Tim was waiting for them in the yard when they got back. His eyes lit up at the sight of Lou looking flushed and happy. "You enjoyed yourselves then?" he asked.

"We had a great time!" Lou agreed enthusiastically as she dismounted and led Spirit into his box.

It didn't take long for them to rub the horses down. Amy stood talking to Tim while Lou finished off. As Lou stepped out of Spirit's box, Mistral's head appeared over her door. Lou walked across to where Amy and Tim were waiting and, once again, Amy noticed Mistral's eyes following her. Then, to Amy's amazement, Mistral lifted her head slightly and let out a long, deep nicker.

There was no doubt about it, Mistral was actually calling to Lou!

Chapter Six

"Of course I don't mind helping you with Mistral," said Lou to Amy later that afternoon. "Although I don't see what I can do. And don't forget, Scott will be back in a couple of days and we'll be leaving then."

"That will be fine," Amy told her. She crossed her fingers behind her back and hoped that two days would be long enough for her to work out why Mistral responded to Lou and no one else. She was sure it would provide her with the key to unlocking the mare's problems.

The door opened and Helena came out carrying Lily. "Hello," she said, as she noticed Amy sitting on the cane chair. "We were just talking about you."

"You were?" asked Amy in surprise.

"Yes, we were just saying how much Amy likes to ride, weren't we, Lily?" said Helena to the little girl who had her fingers tangled in her mother's curly hair

Amy smiled at Lily. "Do you like horses, Lily?"

Lily turned her face into Helena's chest. "Come on silly," Helena said, rubbing her back.

Amy felt a little frustrated, but she tried again. "Hey, Lily," she said softly.

Lily turned her head slightly and looked at Amy.

"Do you like horses?" Amy repeated.

Lily slowly nodded her head and then smiled brightly at

Amy, who felt her heart skip. It was the first time since she had arrived that Lily had smiled at her. Maybe there was hope that her baby sister would come to bond with her after all.

When Amy woke the next morning she remembered her promise to help Emma with Caspian. She realized, with a sinking feeling, that she should try and seek her out sometime during the day. Ordinarily, she would have enjoyed sharing her knowledge, but Emma didn't want her help and that made it very awkward.

Amy pulled on her clothes and tied back her hair before heading down to the yard. She thought at first that she was the only one up and about, but as she approached Caspian's stable she heard Emma's voice. She was talking to Caspian as she groomed him.

"Hi," said Amy, looking over the top of the door.

"Hello," said Emma brusquely, not even pausing in her long sweeping strokes.

"You're here early," Amy commented.

"I've got a lot to do," Emma replied, refusing to be drawn into conversation.

Amy decided to give it one last shot. "Do you want a hand with that?"

"I'm just finishing up," Emma declared and packed the stable rubber into the grooming tray. She turned to face Amy. "I guess this means that you're here to help with Caspian."

"Dad was probably just thinking that I could show you some of the things we do at Heartland, that's all," Amy said.

Emma held her hands in the air and said in a sarcastic tone, "Believe me, we've all heard about the things you do at Heartland."

Amy could feel her cheeks growing warm. Before she could answer, Emma nodded towards the bottle she was holding. "Is that for Caspian?"

"It's a Bach Flower Remedy," Amy replied. "There are thirty-eight different remedies which can be used on their own or blended together. Since Caspian lives on his nerves, I thought we could try to restore his balance by using Impatiens and Aspen. They're particularly useful for calming nervous animals that anticipate things the way Caspian does." She unscrewed the lid of the bottle, "You need to put a few drops..."

"...into his water," Emma finished for her.

Amy looked at her with surprise.

"Lucky guess," Emma shrugged.

Amy held out the bottle. "You can also add it to his feed, or use it with a pump and spray the air in the loose box," she told her. "You might like to try lavender on him, too. It's a great relaxant," she went on. "Mix it with some witch hazel and warm water, then wipe it over his face, neck, legs and spine with a sponge."

"How long will it take before we see a difference?" Emma asked curiously.

Amy tried not to look surprised at Emma's sudden display of interest. "Sometimes they can work quite quickly. Hopefully, by the end of the week you'll start to see a small change in him," she replied. "But sometimes it's more gradual, and you're looking at months, not weeks." The girls were interrupted by Lou, calling for Amy.

"Sorry," Amy apologized.

"It's OK, I'd heard enough anyway," Emma responded abruptly.

Amy sighed inwardly as she let herself out of the loose box. Just as she had begun to think that Emma was thawing towards her, the other girl had returned to her usual offhand manner.

Amy's expression brightened at the sight of her sister leaning over the loose-box door looking at Mistral.

"She's very pretty," Lou observed as Amy joined her.

"She is, and you can tell by the way she moves that she would be incredible to ride," Amy replied.

Mistral snorted and edged backwards until her tail touched the far wall.

"Does she always do that when people are around?" Lou frowned.

"She's never shown any enjoyment in human company – until she saw you," said Amy, sliding back the bolt on the stable door.

"Do you have any idea why?" Lou asked.

Amy soothed Mistral before leading her from the box. "Well, I've been thinking about that, and the only reason I've been able to come up with is that the fact that the couple of times you've been around Mistral, you've ignored her."

Lou half-closed her eyes in concentration. "I guess I have," she said slowly. "I was more interested in Spirit because I'd heard so much about him from Helena."

"Well, whatever the reason, it's given me a clue to what we should try doing with her," said Amy as they made their way down to the ring. "I think that Mistral must have had some kind of bad experience in her past where she was pressured into doing something she wasn't ready for. I can't work out what it could be because she's not supposed to have had any real training yet. But if I'm right, then I think Mistral might be happier working with you."

"I don't understand," Lou ran her hand through her hair. "Surely the moment I start working with her she'll just see me as pressuring her, too?"

"I've thought about that," Amy admitted. "But horses work on a different level from us. They do react to what they see and hear, like we do, but they also react a great deal to what they sense. I think that Mistral senses you are different from everyone else she's met so far. Everyone who's been with her since she's arrived has been one hundred per cent focused on the horses here and getting the best results out of them – and that includes me. But you're not. It took days before you even came and looked at the horses!"

Lou smiled ruefully. "I guess you're right," she acknowledged. "It's not that I didn't want to be with the horses, it's just that I was so anxious to get to know Lily and Helena."

"Exactly, whereas Mistral sensed that my priority, like everyone else's here, is the horses," Amy finished.

Lou nodded her head slowly. "It does make sense," she said.

"But you'll have to tell me exactly what to do."

"Of course," Amy agreed. "And I'm hoping that soon I'll be working with her, too. We just need to convince her that being with us can be fun." As she walked across to take up her position on the fence, Amy thought about the secret hope which she hadn't shared with Lou – that by helping a strong, proud horse like Mistral work through her difficulties, Lou would fully regain her own confidence with horses at last.

Lou had done join-up back at Heartland but Amy noticed that she was nervous. Even from where she sat, Amy could see Lou's white knuckles as she clenched Mistral's lead rope. "Relax," she called across. "Let her go and send her to the outside of the ring, just like you've done before."

Lou nodded and set her jaw in the determined expression that Amy often wore. As she sent Mistral to the ringside, Helena and Tim approached from the ranch. The black mare shied slightly as they climbed on to the fence and Lou instinctively took a step back. Go on, Lou, Amy willed her silently. She knew that it was important for Lou to deal with this on her own, so that her confidence would grow. Lou hesitated for just a moment before re-taking her stance and calling out sharply, "Mistral, move on!" The black horse snorted and immediately swerved back on to the track.

Tim and Helena sat either side of Amy. "We thought we'd come down and see how you were getting on with Mistral," Tim told her. "Lou's got her going nicely."

It was true, Amy thought, Mistral was cantering steadily

with her neck arched and her tail raised. She was relaxed and showed none of the tension of previous sessions.

"I've been telling Helena of my plan to start join-up with my youngsters," Tim commented. "Can you explain to her what Lou's doing?"

"Sure." Amy shifted her position slightly and began to explain, "The purpose of joining-up with a horse is to encourage it to choose to be with you, rather than trying to force it to work with you. Lou will drive Mistral away from her until she sees signs that the horse wants to join her. See?" she pointed at Mistral. "She's doing it now." Mistral's head was lowered and she was opening and closing her mouth. "Mistral's telling Lou that she no longer wants to run away from her," Amy went on. "In a moment, Lou will turn her shoulders, so she's no longer in an aggressive stance, and allow Mistral to come and join her in the centre of the ring."

As Amy was speaking, Lou did exactly that and Amy felt a wave of pride as Mistral walked across to her sister. Lou didn't look at the horse. Instead she walked to the perimeter of the ring and, without hesitation, Mistral followed her. Wherever Lou went, the mare followed, showing that she had put her trust and confidence in Lou and wanted to be her friend.

Amy felt a little choked with emotion. Seeing a horse joining-up was an incredibly powerful experience.

"Wow," said Helena softly. "I've never seen anything like it."

Amy cleared her throat. "We use join-up to begin a partnership based on trust, rather than domination, with the horse."

As Helena nodded, Amy slipped from the fence and walked across to Mistral. "Well done," she smiled at her sister whose cheeks were flushed.

"I can't believe I did it!" Lou exclaimed, "She was so good."

Lou quietly stroked Mistral's forehead while Amy clipped on the lunge line. "Just take it steadily," Amy said. "She needs to feel your confidence, so make sure everything you do is sure and controlled, OK?"

"What if she doesn't behave? What if she bucks or rears?" There was no mistaking the anxiety in Lou's voice.

"I'll be there straightaway," Amy promised. "Just remember – reward good behaviour, ignore bad behaviour."

Lou nodded and raised the lunging whip to form a triangle between herself and Mistral. Then Lou called out in a firm voice for the mare to walk on.

Amy crossed her fingers and watched. To her own amazement, Mistral walked calmly forward. With her long black mane blowing in the slight breeze, and her thick tail kinked out behind her, she looked like she should be a movie horse, Amy thought.

"Trot," Lou called, giving the whip the slightest of flicks on the ground and Mistral immediately sprang forward. She broke into a canter in the corner of the ring and Amy experienced an anxious moment, but Lou brought her back to a walk before sending her forward, once again, into a beautiful balanced trot. After ten minutes, Amy signalled to Lou to bring the session to an end and went over to congratulate her sister. They were soon joined by Helena and Tim.

"You were brilliant!" Tim exclaimed, spontaneously hugging Lou. "Well done, both of you! That's the most we've ever had out of her," he enthused, turning to pat Mistral. The big black horse rolled her eyes and stepped backwards. "Steady, girl," Tim soothed. "There's still a lot of work to be done," he said to Amy, "but you've made a tremendous breakthrough today. I'd started to think about selling her on, but seeing her working like that has made me hopeful we can make something of her yet."

"That was great," Helena squeezed Lou's arm. Then she glanced at her watch. "I'd better get back to the house, I promised Caro I'd only be away for ten minutes! She's watching Lily for me."

"I'll come with you," Lou offered. "You don't need me to do anything else do you, Amy?"

"No, thanks," Amy answered quietly and took the lead rope from Lou. "I'd better walk Mistral back up to the yard and rub her down." She patted the mare's neck gently before clicking to her to walk on. She was aware that she should feel more pleased with Lou's success. But she was struggling with the feeling that she wasn't needed at her father's ranch. *Maybe I should have stayed at Heartland with Ty and Grandpa. It's there that I'm really needed*, she thought.

Her eyes stung with tears, and feeling frustrated with herself, Amy blinked them away. She tried to think more positively as she rummaged in her pocket and pulled out a mint for Mistral. The mare cautiously lipped it off her hand. "That's a good girl," Amy stroked the horse's warm neck. "You did well today. The next step is for you to learn to put your trust in me, too."

Before schooling Spirit the next day, Amy spent a long time in his stall doing T-touch. She hoped that it would help Spirit bond with her. As the grey horse turned to look at her through large brown eyes, he blew heavily. Amy smiled and he rested his head on her shoulder. "Hey, the idea's not to relax you so much you go to sleep!" she said, laughing and moving away.

Spirit's ears pricked up at the sound of hooves clattering in the yard. Amy looked out and saw Emma leading Caspian towards his box. Her hair was falling in untidy strands about her face and one side of her jodhpurs was caked in mud. She had obviously taken a fall.

Amy hurried out. "Are you OK? Do you want me to take him for you?" she asked with concern.

Caspian had foam flecks on his chest and was dancing agitatedly on his toes. Emma didn't say anything. "What happened?" Amy persisted.

Emma rounded on her. "I've had enough of your help, thank you. Just let me handle my horse in my own way, OK? If your methods are so great, why aren't you getting anywhere with Spirit and Mistral? Just leave me alone!"

Leaving Amy standing with her mouth open in amazement, Emma pulled Caspian forward and slammed the door of his box shut behind them.

Fine, Amy thought angrily. *If that's the way you want it, then that's all right with me.* She walked back into Spirit's stall, trying hard to control her anger. She felt more determined than ever to help Mistral and Spirit and prove that Heartland's methods, her methods, really did work. Deftly she tacked up Spirit and led him down to the ring.

Although Spirit still wasn't the same horse that Amy had watched on the video, there was a slight improvement during his session. Usually he tipped the top poles of his jumps, but this time he cleared every one with a few inches to spare.

"Well done!" Amy said, and patted his neck as they finished the circuit. She glanced at her watch. She had just enough time to get him back to his loose box, before taking Mistral down to the ring to meet Lou.

Lou was waiting in the centre of the ring when Amy got back. Mistral pricked her ears forward as soon as she noticed her. Amy handed the mare over to be lunged, hoping fervently that Mistral would work without getting stressed – it was essential if Amy's plan for her was to be put into action.

Amy watched Lou put the mare through various transitions on the lunging line. The horse went from a fluid canter to a trot before walking calmly round the track.

"That's great! Now try her on the other rein," Amy called.

Lou nodded and skilfully sent Mistral in the other direction. Amy looked at Lou's bright blue eyes, focused on the horse, and realized how much her sister's confidence was increasing.

"She's working well for you," Amy congratulated her sister as she brought Mistral to a halt.

"She's amazing," Lou said enthusiastically. "I'm going to miss working with her."

Amy frowned slightly, then suddenly realized what her sister meant. "Of course, Scott's coming back tomorrow!" Amy declared.

Lou nodded, her eyes lighting up. "I can't wait to see him," she admitted. "But I'm starting to understand how difficult it was for you to leave your work at Heartland. It's going to be hard leaving Mistral – wondering about her progress and wondering what I could have done with her if I was here."

Amy felt a surge of delight. She had hoped that riding Spirit would help to restore her sister's confidence and love of horses. But it seemed Lou's work with Mistral had achieved even more. Lou was beginning to experience the bond that could develop between horse and healer.

"What you've done so far with Mistral is great," Amy said. "I think you've begun to help her understand that being with people can be good – not stressful. I think she's ready for me to try something else with her now."

A look of curiosity passed across Lou's face. "What?" she asked curiously.

"Wait and see," Amy teased. "First of all, though, I need to make sure that she's happy with me lunging her, too."

Amy took over the lunging line and clicked to Mistral. The mare swivelled her ear towards the sound of Amy's voice. "Trot on," Amy called reassuringly and watched with delight as, without a trace of anxiety, Mistral obeyed her command.

Amy worked Mistral for five minutes on each rein and then

brought her back into the centre of the ring. She had spent hours with Mistral over the last couple of days, not just joining-up with her but also doing T-touch and massage with essential oils. She was sure that the mare was now ready to be taken on to the next stage in her training. Crossing her fingers, Amy walked across to the gate of the school and collected the saddle and bridle she had brought down earlier.

"You're going to try and ride her?" Lou asked in surprise.

"Nope, I'm just going to introduce her to the tack and, as long as she's happy wearing it, then tomorrow I'll lunge her tacked up," Amy explained.

Mistral was looking at the tack with her ears back. "It's OK, girl," Amy soothed. She made sure that the girth was over the saddle and the stirrup irons were secured at the top of their leathers so that nothing could bang against Mistral and give her a fright. She then placed the saddle gently on to Mistral's withers before running it down into position on her back. Mistral's muscles tensed, but she remained still as Amy slowly reached the girth around and fastened it into position.

"Good girl," Amy praised, and she gave Mistral a mint to crunch on. The mare lipped it off her palm and Amy was pleased to see that she was showing none of the panic she when lunged for the first time. Mistral's face looked a little tense, her nostrils were slightly flared, but there was something in her eyes that Amy couldn't quite understand. The mare looked as if she knew what was going on. She didn't have the nervous look of a horse experiencing something new and strange.

Amy frowned.

"She's doing well, isn't she?" Lou commented.

"Almost too well," said Amy slowly.

"How can she do too well?" Lou asked in surprise. "She's just responding to the work that we've put in on her, surely?"

"It would be nice to think so, but somehow, I'm pretty sure it's not the case," Amy replied. She looked at Mistral, who was standing quietly. The behaviour just didn't make sense — her dislike of people, her terrified reaction to being lunged, and now her complete lack of surprise at a saddle and bridle.

Amy picked up the bridle and slowly passed the reins over the mare's head. As she placed the bit against Mistral's teeth, she immediately opened her mouth and accepted it.

"I thought so," Amy said wonderingly.

"What?" Lou asked puzzled.

"Whoever sold Mistral to Dad lied!" Amy exclaimed. "He bought her unbacked, but she's worn a saddle and a bridle before. I'm sure of it!"

Chapter Seven

"You've actually managed to put a saddle and bridle on Mistral?" Tim asked, turning away from the fish on the grill to look at Amy and Lou in amazement.

"Yes," Amy nodded.

"How did she react to that?" Tim looked astonished.

"To be honest, she acted like she'd done it all before," Amy told him.

"Amy's got an interesting theory," said Lou, setting down a pile of plates on the table.

Tim smiled encouragingly at Amy.

"I was just wondering," said Amy. "Well, more than wondering, really. I'm sure Mistral has already been backed. Do you mind if I use your office and look through the records this afternoon?"

"Of course you can. What is it you're hoping to find?" Tim asked with interest.

"I don't know yet – just any clue to Mistral's history, I guess," Amy replied. She turned and saw Helena standing with her arm around Lou's shoulders. The two of them were chatting and laughing happily and once again Amy felt a little isolated.

After a few moments she quietly slipped away to the top paddock, where Mistral and Spirit were grazing along with Jinx and Lace. She climbed on to the top bar of the fence and rested her chin in her hand.

Her thoughts drifted to the time her father had visited Heartland. Amy realized she was starting to understand a little of what her sister must have felt, when she had struggled to bond with Tim during his visit, while Amy had got along with him so well. Here in Australia she saw Lou earning her father's praise, and being loved by Helena and Lily, while, she felt, her own achievements were being taken for granted. *Lou had Dad for so much longer than I did when we were growing up, it's not surprising she's closer to him than I am*, Amy thought unhappily. Immediately it struck her that, of course, Lily would have their father for the whole of her childhood, too.

She was so wrapped up in her thoughts that she didn't hear her father walk up behind her. "Lunch is ready," he said quietly.

"I'm not really hungry," Amy replied.

"Are you all right?" Tim asked.

"Sure," Amy said, forcing a smile on to her face as she slipped off the fence. "I'm just really keen to find out more about Mistral's background, that's all."

"OK. As long as you're sure," Tim told her. "I'd better get back to the barbecue before the fish are cremated," he joked.

Amy watched him go, then made her way to the stable block and let herself into his office. She figured that one way of forgetting her problems was to try and fix Mistral's.

The inside of the office was painted in neutral cream and coffee colours and a huge potted palm tree flourished in one corner. One wall was taken up with filing cabinets and Amy decided to begin her search with them. Each drawer was ordered by date, so she pulled out the bottom drawer of the end cabinet. Inside, everything was alphabetically sorted and Amy had no difficulty locating Mistral's file.

She took the slim green folder across to her father's desk and settled herself comfortably in his deep leather chair. A collection of photographs grouped in one corner of the desk caught her eye and she paused in her search to look at them. There was one of Tim and Helena on their wedding day. It was beautiful, but Amy's stomach lurched as she looked at it. The only bride she had ever envisaged her father with was her mother – it hurt to see him laughing into Helena's eyes as they cut their wedding cake. She quickly glanced at the next photo and smiled to see a very young Lou, with her hair in plaits, dressed in a formal school uniform. It must have been her first day at school in England, Amy realized. She ran her eye over the next few pictures – photos of horses her father had owned – and then came to the last frame, which contained three small photos of Lily. There was one of Lily as a newborn, looking all red and wrinkled as she lay in Helena's arms, engulfed by a white blanket. In the next one she was asleep with a teddy bear, tiny fingers clutching tightly to one paw. And the third was a recent shot, taken of Lily on her swing, her brown eyes sparkling and her chestnut curls tumbling over her cheeks.

Amy felt a sharp stab of pain. There was no photograph of her! She quickly scanned the rest of the room but there was no picture of her anywhere. She drew in a deep breath. *It doesn't matter*, she told herself, but she knew that it did. It mattered to her more deeply than she could put into words.

Quickly she opened up Mistral's file to try and take her mind off the photographs but, as she leafed through the shipping bills, veterinary and insurance certificates, all that kept going through her head was, *Why doesn't Dad have a photograph of me?*

She located the piece of paper that she had been looking for, which was the bill of sale from Mistral's last yard. She reached for the phone and dialled the number written at the top of the page. A voice answered in Spanish, but the moment Amy spoke, the receptionist switched to heavily accented but excellent English. Amy briefly explained who she was and asked to speak to Mistral's ex-owner.

"I'm so sorry but he isn't here at the moment. Perhaps you would like to speak with the manager instead?"

"Thank you," Amy said politely and waited until a deep, male voice came on to the line.

As Amy began to describe the problems they were having with Mistral, the manager interrupted her brusquely. "You looked over the horse and she was fine. You had a full veterinary inspection which she passed. You cannot send her back."

"We don't want to send her back," said Amy quickly. "I was just trying to find out if she had any experience in your yard that might have made her afraid of people."

"Are you trying to say that we don't treat our horses well?" the man said indignantly. "We have the finest of reputations! The horse you have from us was one of our best. She was very good for us here. She had excellent prospects – she was clearing over one and a half metres before she left."

"Over one and a half metres? But she was sold as unbacked!" Amy exclaimed.

There was a long pause and Amy wondered if they had been cut off, but then the manager spoke again. "She was sold as a youngster only," he said. "I have to go, I am a very busy man. I'm sorry I cannot help you any more."

There was a click as he hung up, but it didn't matter. He had given Amy the information she needed. She now knew why it was that Mistral didn't like human company and didn't want to work. She had been backed and schooled at too young an age. The fact that she had been clearing one and a half metres indicated that Mistral had been given too much to do too soon. It was, Amy thought, the equivalent of asking a small child to do algebra while still in nursery. Mistral could well have suffered something of a breakdown. It was not surprising she now had a mental block about people and being trained. She had allowed them to put a bridle and saddle on her, which meant that they were already moving in the right direction, but Mistral also needed persuading that learning was fun and easy. Maybe then Amy could undo the damage that had been done.

As Amy left her father's office, her cellphone began to ring. Ty's number came up on the screen and she smiled as she answered. "Hello," she said.

"How are things?" his familiar voice asked.

"OK, thanks. I've just discovered something about Mistral — the horse I'm working with." As Amy told Ty about her phone conversation, she felt a rush of happiness. It was almost like being back at Heartland, she thought, where she and Ty always discussed the horses' problems.

"So you want to make learning fun?" Ty mused. "You could try putting a toy in her stable for a start."

"I was thinking that," Amy replied enthusiastically. "I know they're often used to stop stabled horses from getting bored, but I thought that if I could start getting Mistral interested in playing – and develop her sense of curiosity – it would really help her." She paused for a moment, then continued. "It's good to talk to you. How are things going back at home?"

"Good, thanks. Marnie's really enjoying herself, although she reckons she hasn't got 'city hands' any more. She's finally given up the battle to keep her nails long," Ty laughed and Amy closed her eyes to listen to the sound. "Jack's been great. He's sharing the cooking with Marnie and he's keeping the business side of things ticking over. Soraya is coming up each day to help with the exercising. She told me to tell you that Sundance is keeping fit but missing you. Ben and I are doing just fine."

"Really?" Amy asked.

"Really," Ty replied firmly. "Now, how about you?"

Amy hesitated and then confided in Ty about her continuing struggle to fit in.

"I thought you decided you were going to work at it after we last spoke?" Ty queried gently.

Amy sighed. "I've tried, but it's all so different from Heartland," she said. "And I can't help feeling that everyone's interested in Lou and I'm like the invisible sister – even down to the fact that Dad doesn't keep a photo of me on his desk." But even as she spoke, a small voice in her head said, *You haven't really tried to join in, not in the same way that Lou has.*

She tried not to listen to it and to focus on Ty's reply instead. "I know it will all work out for you eventually, you've just got to give it time," he told her reassuringly.

Amy agreed and said her goodbyes. As she hung up she realized that her time at the ranch was passing quickly. If she wasn't careful, she'd be going home nearly as much of a stranger to her dad's new family as when she arrived.

Amy rummaged around in the black bins in the tack room. There were mountains of spare leading reins, rubber reins, martingales and halters but she finally managed to find a green cylindrical canister. Feeling pleased, she went into the adjoining feed room, unscrewed the top of the canister and filled it with some pony nuts.

She took the toy into Mistral's loose box and encouraged her to sniff it before she put it down on the floor. The mare blew heavily through her nostrils at the toy, then ignored it completely. Amy felt a little disappointed, but she knew that it wasn't realistic to expect a horse like Mistral to begin rolling it about on the floor immediately. "The only way you can get the treats to fall out of the holes is by pushing the toy with your nose," Amy explained to the mare. "I want it empty by tomorrow morning," she added sternly. Then she patted Mistral gently and slipped out of the door.

By the time the evening meal was ready, Amy's stomach was rumbling from her missed lunch. She ate her way through the delicious stew that Tim had made and listened to Lou and

Helena chat about their afternoon. They had taken Lily swimming in a local pool, and spent some time in the gym while Lily played in the nursery.

Amy was fairly quiet throughout the meal until Tim turned to her. "Did you manage to find out anything about Mistral?" he asked interestedly.

Amy briefly told him what she had discovered.

"That's quite unbelievable," Tim said incredulously. "They had her jumping over one and a half metres, you say?"

Amy nodded.

"I must phone Pete – that's my business partner in England – and let him know," Tim commented. "Well done, Amy. It certainly explains Mistral's behaviour."

Despite Tim's praise, Amy couldn't make herself meet his eyes and as soon as she could she made her excuses and escaped from the table. She didn't feel she could ask her father why it was he didn't have her photo on his desk, but it was something she really needed to know. It was hard to act normally around him when she was feeling so left out.

When Amy let herself into Mistral's box the next morning, to her amazement the big black horse actually walked over to her and nuzzled her hand. Barely containing her delight, Amy quickly drew a horse cookie out of her pocket and fed it to her. She then slowly bent down and shook the toy she had left out the night before. It was empty! "You played with your toy!" Amy exclaimed in delight.

She gave Mistral a thorough grooming and led her down to

the ring. Lou hadn't arrived so Amy spent half an hour lunging the mare fully tacked. The horse responded well and Amy knew that Mistral was finally learning to trust people again.

She decided to have some fun. She sent Mistral out to the side of the ring and began the process of join-up. Fairly quickly, the mare lowered her head and began to look as if she were chewing air. Amy turned her body away from Mistral to encourage her to come and join her.

The moment Amy sensed the horse behind her, she moved away. Mistral followed and Amy moved faster. The mare moved after her again and Amy broke into a jog. Mistral quickened her pace until she was trotting after Amy. Amy stopped and rewarded her with a horse cookie, then moved off again. She jogged around from spot to spot, with the mare chasing her, until finally she stopped, breathless and laughing, and gave the horse a last reward. For the first time Mistral didn't stiffen as she patted her.

"She's coming on well," Lou called, walking over to greet them.

"She is, isn't she?" Amy replied, grinning.

"I'm glad to see you looking happier," Lou commented. "You seemed quite down last night."

"Did I?" Amy said non-committally. She walked across to the fence to collect Mistral's tack.

"You were very quiet," Lou persisted.

"Oh, I was probably just thinking about what to do with Mistral today," Amy said dismissively, and felt relieved when Lou dropped the subject.

"What are you going to do with her now?" Lou asked.

Amy grinned. "I think she's ready for me to sit on her," she told Lou.

A worried frown creased Lou's forehead. "I don't know, Amy, she's still unpredictable. Are you sure?"

Amy tried to remain patient. "I know what I'm doing," she said calmly. "All you have to do is boost me up so I can drape myself over Mistral's back. If she reacts in a frightened way, I can slip off immediately without getting hurt, OK?"

Lou agreed. "But if she shows any sign of misbehaving, you'll slip straight off, OK?"

"I promise," Amy said, tightening the chin strap on her hat before standing beside Mistral. She raised her lower leg and Lou gently boosted her over the saddle. Amy hung quietly over Mistral's back. The mare snorted nervously and took two steps back. Amy kept still and called soothingly, "Steady, girl. Steady." Mistral blew long and loud out through her nostrils but stood still.

"What now?" Lou asked, barely raising her voice above a whisper.

"I want you to do a little bit of T-touch on her so that she relaxes," Amy replied. "Then, when she does, I want you to lead her forward a few steps – just a few steps – then stop and reward her, then lead her a few steps more," Amy explained.

After several minutes, Amy felt the horse's muscles unknot and Lou said, "I'm going to lead her forward now."

Mistral took three steps before Lou stopped and patted her gently.

"Go further now. I think she's going to be all right," Amy said quietly.

As Lou began to walk round the ring, Amy carefully inched her leg over Mistral's quarters and slowly sat up in the saddle. Mistral swivelled one ear back at her, but kept the other pricked forward happily. After they had completed one circuit of the ring, Lou halted and Amy gently dismounted.

"Wow!" Lou exclaimed in delight. "I can't believe that we've got her so far before I go away!"

Amy nodded and rubbed the mare between the eyes gently. "You're doing brilliantly, girl," she told Mistral and dropped a kiss on her satiny nose.

When Amy led Spirit down to the jumping arena later that day, she was still glowing from her success with Mistral. She began to warm Spirit up by asking him to trot round the perimeter of the ring. Soon she was sure that the horse was picking up on some of her happiness. His paces were smoother and more confident and, as Amy set him at the first jump, she felt him give a rush of pleasure for the first time. His paces became elevated, his neck arched proudly, and he pushed eagerly against the bit.

"OK, boy, it's just you and me," she whispered.

Spirit collected himself and flew over the first jump as if he had wings. Amy laughed aloud at his enthusiasm. As she concentrated on the second jump, the grey suddenly missed his stride and called out loudly. Amy frowned and glanced round to see what had distracted him. She saw that Helena and Lou were walking along the path between the arena and the ranch. Amy tried to collect Spirit and set him at the fence again, but his concentration was gone and he sent poles flying everywhere.

Annoyed and frustrated, Amy gave up trying to regain the momentum she had lost, and walked Spirit out of the arena instead. Despondency crept over her as she realized that she had completely underestimated the bond between Spirit and Helena. She couldn't ever remember seeing a horse respond so strongly to another person before.

"Oh, Amy, I'm so sorry," Helena said, hurrying over. "We've just come back from taking Lily for a walk and I didn't think you'd be working with Spirit."

"It's fine," said Amy shortly, trying hard not to show her frustration, but knowing that she wasn't succeeding. Helena looked wretched and her cheeks were slightly flushed, but Amy refused to say anything to make her feel better. She felt Helena should have known not to risk appearing around Spirit when she was working with him. If she had made a breakthrough with the horse, then Helena had effectively ruined it all.

"Amy?" Lou called after her as she rode off. Amy could see her sister's puzzled frown, but she didn't care.

Then a window at the back of the ranch suddenly opened and Tim stuck his head out. "Hey!" he called to Lou. "You have a visitor who's very keen to see you!"

Lou's concerned expression was replaced with one of joy as she realized who her father meant. "Scott's back!" she exclaimed, and she and Helena headed up to the ranch.

* * *

Just as Amy was turning the handle of her bedroom door, Lou came up the stairs. "I'm just going to give Lily her bath. Will you help me?" she asked Amy.

"Actually Lou, I was planning to have an early night tonight. I've got to be up early tomorrow," Amy told her.

"Oh, come on, Amy, who are you trying to kid?" Lou replied, taking Amy by surprise. "What is wrong with you? You don't try and join in with anything, you don't want to have anything to do with Lily, you're offhand with Helena when all she tries to do is make you feel like part of the family. You're even being cool towards Dad after he's bent over backwards to make you feel at home here. I just don't understand why you're being like this."

Amy's mouth dropped open. How could Lou be so insensitive to how she was feeling? "Oh, forget it," she said feeling a surge of frustration, "I might have known you wouldn't understand."

"What's that supposed to mean?" Lou snapped.

"Although you might have," Amy continued, "considering how left out you felt when Dad came to stay with us at Heartland!"

There was a long pause. Both sisters stared at each other. "Are you saying that you don't feel as if you fit in?" Lou asked, looking bewildered.

"Yes, Lou, that's exactly how I feel, but don't worry because it won't be long before I'm back at Heartland, where I do!" Amy retorted, and she stormed into her bedroom and slammed the door behind her.

Chapter Eight

With trembling fingers, Amy pressed Ty's number into her phone. He answered it on the third ring. "Amy?" he answered, sounding surprised.

"Hi, how are you?" Amy asked, aware that her voice was flat.

"Everything's good here," Ty told her. "You don't sound like your normal self, though. Is everything OK?"

Amy felt her heart lighten a little at the sound of concern in Ty's voice. He understood her so well. "I'm starting to wish I hadn't come," she admitted, lying back on her bed and staring up at the ceiling. "At least if I'd stayed at home I would have been useful. I'd have been able to take some work off you."

"I've been fine," Ty told her. "Really. I'm just sorry to hear it isn't all going so well for you."

"I haven't managed to do anything right since I came here," Amy wailed. "If it hadn't been for Lou working with Mistral, then I might never have made a breakthrough. Tim and Helena think Lou is fantastic – and Lily loves her as well and always calls for her, but doesn't want to have anything to do with me. I feel like Lou's more a part of their family now than mine. Emma can't stand being around me – I know she'd have been a lot happier if I hadn't come."

As she took a breath, Ty interrupted. "Hey, Amy, this isn't like you."

"What do you mean?" Amy asked. She had been expecting Ty to support her.

"Well, you usually love to join in and get involved. It's not like you to isolate yourself."

"But I feel so left out here," Amy wailed.

"Yes, but I think maybe that's because you've spent too much time getting to know the horses and not enough time getting to know the people," Ty suggested.

Amy had to admit it was probably true. "Horses are just so much easier," she said quietly.

Ty laughed, then his voice became gentle. "Amy, I think that you went to Australia with the wrong expectations. It's like you expected everyone out there to see you and treat you the same way that we do at Heartland. But to them you're Lily's big sister and Tim's daughter. Maybe if you tried seeing yourself that way, you might be happier. Who knows, you might even find it easier to fit in."

Amy took a while to think over what Ty was saying. It wasn't what she'd wanted to hear but she had a feeling he might be right.

Ty must have guessed that she was struggling with emotions because he said quietly, "Just think about it, OK? And get an early night. You sound tired. Everything will seem better in the morning."

"Thanks, Ty," said Amy in a small voice. "Give my love to Grandpa."

"I will," Ty promised. "And remember, we all love you here. They will in Australia, too, if you let them get to know you."

Amy lay on her bed with her head on her arms, thinking over what Ty had said to her. But she was so tired that, before long, she had fallen asleep.

When Amy walked up from the stables the following morning, she was surprised to see Scott stowing bags in the back of a green jeep.

"I rented it for the week," he explained.

"I didn't think you'd be leaving this early," said Amy, looking around for Lou. She knew she couldn't let her leave without making up with her first.

"We've got a lot of travelling to do. We're heading out to Alice Springs, then on to visit Uluru."

"Uluru?" Amy frowned.

"It's the Aboriginal name for Ayers Rock – apparently it means 'great pebble'," Scott explained with a grin.

A movement on the veranda caught Amy's eye and she turned to see Lou struggling with two rucksacks. "Here," Amy said, jogging across to help.

"Thanks," said Lou glancing up at her.

Amy read the expression in her eyes and sensed that Lou wanted to make up their argument as much as she did. "I'm sorry," said Amy softly. "I guess I haven't made much of an effort to join in."

"I'm sorry, too," Lou smiled. "At least you've got time to sort things out while I'm gone. Get to know Lily. She's your sister as much as mine – and she'll love you, I know she will. And try to relax with Helena. She's not looking to be a replacement mother to us — just a friend. You know what?" Lou looked thoughtful. "I think Mom would have liked her."

Amy nodded her head before shouldering the rucksack and walking across to the jeep with Lou. "I spoke with Ty on the phone last night and he told me to stop thinking of myself as 'Heartland's Amy' and start seeing myself as part of the family, instead."

"That's good advice," Lou said, nodding, as she placed her bag in the back of the jeep.

"What is?" Scott asked, tipping his sunglasses down on to the bridge of his nose and peering over at them.

"Being nice to sisters!" Lou laughed as she and Amy hugged one another.

"I said goodbye to Dad, Helena and Lily when you were down in the yard," Lou told Amy. "They've gone to an auction with Pat. Helena asked me to tell you that there's some freshly baked muffins in the oven for your breakfast."

Scott started the engine and Lou slid into the passenger seat.

"Have a great time," Amy called through the window.

"See you next week!" Lou replied and waved as the jeep rolled away.

Amy waved back until her sister had disappeared from sight, fighting the sudden wave of loneliness that swept over her.

Amy decided that the best thing she could do was go for a long ride on Spirit. She needed time to mull over Lou's words. Deciding she could have breakfast later, she headed back down to the yard. Emma was outside Caspian's loose box talking to

Caro. Amy couldn't help but overhear Emma complaining about having to collect a horse from the airport with Sam.

"I'd love to help you but I need to exercise Jupiter this morning," said Caro, as she stroked the nose of the roan horse that stood in the box next door to Caspian.

Emma sighed. "It's OK, I promised Tim I'd do it. It's just that I could really do with putting in a session with Caspian now that the schooling ring's free."

Amy thought quickly. If she offered to collect the horse, she might help build a bridge between herself and Emma. "I don't mind going if you're busy," she volunteered.

Emma looked taken aback. "Well, if you're sure," she said after a pause. "Sam's expecting to meet me outside the house in a couple of minutes."

"I'll go now, then," Amy told her and, as she turned to retrace her footsteps, she thought she heard Emma mumble, "Thank you," in a low voice.

Sam was just pulling up outside the house as Amy arrived. He looked surprised when she climbed in beside him, but didn't say anything. "I offered to come instead of Emma," she explained.

Sam turned and peered at her for a moment with his sharp blue eyes. Then he grunted and tugged his wide-brimmed hat further down over his face. He let out the clutch and the trailer pulled away down the long sweeping driveway.

Amy leant her forehead against the glass and looked out over the pastures. She was glad to be going with Sam. Since he never felt the need to make conversation, she would be able to sort through her thoughts in peace. Being away from the ranch – even for a couple of hours – was going to do her good, she realized, feeling herself relax. It would give her the distance she needed to put her worries into perspective.

It took an hour to get to the small local airport. During the journey, Amy turned over in her mind everything that Ty and Lou had said to her. The more she considered their advice, the more she felt her guilt over forging a relationship with Helena disappear. Lou's words kept ringing in her ears – *Mom would have liked Helena*. Amy suddenly realized that Helena and her mom would have had a lot in common. *And Mom would have wanted me to have Helena as a friend. It's not as if I'm betraying Mom in any way. She and I couldn't have been closer.* With that last thought, Amy felt the final barrier in her mind lift.

Sam drove around to the holding bay and, for the first time in the journey, he spoke to Amy. "Wait here while I go and sort out the paperwork," he said quietly.

Amy waited patiently until Sam returned for her.

"There," he nodded his head.

Following his gaze, Amy saw a dun-coloured horse being walked up and down. Even from a distance, Amy could see that the horse was frightened. His movements were stiff and unyielding and he repeatedly tossed his head.

She followed Sam over to the groom. "Sorrel tripped and fell when we brought him off the plane," the man explained. "The vet's checked him over and he's fine, but it's unsettled him a little."

Amy ran her eyes over the gelding. He was typical of many of the horses that her father bought in – rough and unconditioned, but with good conformation that an experienced horseman could recognize. "We'll take him from here," said Sam. He looked across at Amy. "You can lead him."

Amy took the leading rope and spoke gently to the horse. She didn't like the closed expression on his face; she had come across it before with frightened horses that had shut themselves off from the outside world and were centred only on their fear.

Amy began to lead Sorrel over to the trailer as Sam brought down the ramp. The horse skittered away nervously and Amy began to doubt that he would load easily.

"Bring him on," Sam told her.

Amy clicked softly and began to walk forward. She felt a surge of relief as he followed after her. The moment his hooves touched the ramp, however, he dug his toes in and refused to go any further. "Come on, boy," Amy encouraged, but when she took another step, he ran backwards, pulling her with him. Amy steadied herself and looked over at Sam who rolled his eyes in exasperation.

"Here," he took the rope from her and tried to lead Sorrel forward. The horse snorted and tossed his head, plunging up and down.

"Do you mind if I try something?" Amy asked.

Sam shrugged and handed Sorrel back to her.

Amy rested her fingers at the base of Sorrel's forelock. She kept her fingers still for a moment so that he could adjust to her touch before she began to work in slow circles. She varied her touch, sometimes pressing her fingers down with a steady pressure and sometimes making circular movements. Eventually, Sorrel began to lower his head and breathe deeply. Amy walked a few steps forwards, but she felt Sorrel tense the moment he reached the ramp. "Could I borrow your necktie, please?" Amy asked Sam.

Sam looked at her and slowly shook his head as if she had made a ridiculous request, but he pulled off the red neckerchief and handed it to Amy. She very gently placed it over Sorrel's eyes so that he couldn't see. "Now you have to depend on me," she whispered to him. "Walk on, there's a good boy. Trust me, you'll be OK."

Sorrel's ears were pricked towards the sound of Amy's voice and as she urged him up on to the ramp, he took four shaky steps and entered the trailer. "Good boy," Amy praised and carefully removed the necktie.

Sam brought up the ramp behind them and Amy smiled as she heard him mutter, "Stone the crows."

She secured Jack before slipping out of the side door and joining Sam.

"Well done," he said gruffly, before turning on the radio to discourage any further conversation.

Amy smiled to herself. Her success with Sorrel, and Sam's grudging praise, had somehow acted as an omen for the remainder of her stay. She believed it was a sign that things were going to change for the better – and she was determined that this time she was going to make every effort to make things work.

There was a welcoming committee at the yard when Amy and Sam arrived. Tim was waiting, along with Pat, Alex, Emma and Caro.

"We're always keen to see the new arrivals," Caro grinned, as she helped Amy to lower the ramp.

Sorrel was going to be Alex's horse so, as soon as the trailer was open, he went inside. Sorrel had calmed down during the journey and he backed obediently down the ramp, but Tim's sharp eyes noticed the dry sweat on his coat.

Sam explained how Amy had calmed Sorrel and covered his eyes to lead him into the trailer. "I didn't think we were going to do it without sedation myself," he admitted.

Tim looked across at Amy. "What made you think of that?" he asked.

Aware that everyone was listening, Amy felt shy as she replied. "Well, since his eyes were covered, he had to rely on me completely and wasn't distracted by any of his surroundings." She shrugged. "It works in the same way as putting blinkers on, I guess. Its just a little more drastic!"

Tim laughed. "You did really well, Amy," he said proudly. "It was a good thing you went!"

He moved in closer to examine the horse and, as he did, Amy noticed the thunderous expression on Emma's face. *Of course*, Amy thought. *Emma was supposed to go and collect Sorrel. Now she thinks that I've tried to go one better than her again.*

Emma turned on her heel and walked off, and Amy decided that her relationship with Emma was going to be the very first thing she worked on. As soon as she could, Amy left the group and went in search of Emma. She found her in the jumping arena, cantering Caspian in circles. Caspian was frothing at the bit and trying to go crabwise rather than straight. Amy could see that he was full of tension that he'd picked up from Emma.

Emma set him at the first jump. Caspian seemed to settle down slightly and he cleared it well. But, as Emma swung him around to face the parallel bars, Amy fell into her line of vision. Seeing her obviously distracted Emma, for Caspian immediately missed his stride and brought down the bars.

Emma tightened her reins and sent him on to the double, which he refused. Looking furious, Emma made Caspian circle tightly and take the jump again – again he refused. Amy couldn't bear to watch Caspian become any more upset. She knew that Emma would never usually jump him like this, and she was afraid of how it would set Caspian's progress back.

Amy took a deep breath. She knew that challenging Emma would antagonize her – but she couldn't bear to watch Caspian getting distressed. She quickly crossed the arena. Emma was attempting the jump for the third time. Again, Caspian swerved away, almost sending Emma over his shoulder this time.

"I think he's picking up on your tension," Amy said. "Do you mind if I try and calm him down a little bit for you?"

Without waiting for an answer she placed her hand gently on Caspian's forehead. Caspian backed away, his eyes rolling. Amy chose a different point and, speaking soothingly to the horse, began to move her fingers in a circular motion. After a few moments, the horse stood still and his breathing became more regular. Amy was concentrating so much on getting Caspian to relax that she didn't notice Emma had dismounted until the girl was standing facing her.

Emma's face was white except for two bright red patches on her cheeks. She spoke in a voice trembling with fury. "I'm sick of this. You come over here so full of yourself, thinking you're above us all with your alternative methods and theories," she snapped. "You're not the only one who can get the best out of horses, you know – even if you think you are. Your dad wouldn't have me here if I didn't get good results."

Amy felt stunned. All she had been trying to do was help. As she took a breath to defend herself, Emma carried on. "All you've done since you came here is take over. I'm really interested in alternative methods but I'd like to have used them to treat Caspian without you constantly butting in. Did you ever think of that? Of course not! Because you never consider other people's feelings." She gave a short, bitter laugh. "Well fine, have Caspian then, since you obviously think you can do better than me!" Emma flung the reins into Amy's hands and began to stalk away across the ring. She then spun on her heel and pointed her finger. "You might know what you're doing around horses, but trust me, you've got a lot to learn when it comes to handling people!"

Chapter Nine

Amy walked Caspian around to cool him off before taking him back to his loose box. She rubbed him down, wondering all the while how she could possibly sort things out with Emma. A shadow fell across the doorway and Amy looked up to see Emma, fiddling nervously with the lead rope that was hanging over the door.

"I'm sorry," Amy and Emma both said at the same time, then half-smiled at each other.

"I shouldn't have yelled at you like that, " Emma apologized.

"And I want you to know that I would never usually treat Caspian that way. I guess I let my own problems cloud my judgement. He deserves better than that." She let herself into the box and Caspian nickered softly before moving across to her. The bond between them was obvious.

"I'm sorry, too," said Amy. "I guess I've been a bit insensitive at times."

Emma raised an eyebrow questioningly.

"The way I took over with Caspian when I first met you," Amy explained.

"I would have preferred it if you'd explained to me that he was frightened, and suggested that I walk out in front of him," Emma admitted.

"I didn't think, sorry," Amy replied sincerely.

Emma nodded. "Over the last couple of days there's been a

definite change in Caspian, though," she said more brightly. "He's not spooking at everything the way he was – and he's not getting over-excited whenever I ask him to go faster than a trot."

"That's great!" Amy felt a rush of delight for Emma.

"But I've probably undone all the good work now," Emma said, looking miserable.

"Of course you haven't," Amy said quickly. "Just spend some time with him now, keep applying the flower remedies and lavender, and I'm sure he'll continue to improve."

"Do you think so?" Emma asked hopefully. She paused and looked a little awkward. "Can show me how to do that massage?" she asked shyly. "I've tried to do it out of a book, but I can't be hitting the right spots because Casp always moves away from my hand."

"Sometimes horses respond better to massage in one area than others. It's a bit like using herbs – they often choose the ones that they want you to use, if you offer them a selection," Amy told her.

"Really?" Emma looked surprised.

Amy nodded and felt a flood of exhilaration; she was finally having a conversation with Emma! "I'm really sorry if you feel I've tried to take over from you since I got here," she said, watching as Emma began to brush some powdered lavender into Caspian's coat.

"I knew deep down that you weren't really," Emma admitted. "It's just that Tim had kept on and on about how you always get such great results from horses, and how I'd be able to learn a lot from you, and I guess I decided I didn't like you before you even arrived."

"My dad said that about me?" Amy's grey eyes widened with surprise.

Emma nodded. "I think he probably said more to me than anyone else, because I've been interested in the methods that you use for a while now. I think Tim thought we'd have a lot in common."

Amy took a brush and worked on Caspian's other side. Emma's earlier attitude towards her was all beginning to make sense now. They worked together in silence for a while. "Why did you sound surprised that your dad should have talked a lot about you?" Emma asked curiously.

Amy sighed. "I guess it's because I've been feeling that I'm not really needed here," she admitted.

Emma looked surprised.

Amy continued moving the brush in long firm strokes. "It's so different from being at home," she went on. "There's always something that needs doing at Heartland. But here, with all the staff that Dad has and the brand new facilities, well, apart from working with Mistral and Spirit there's really nothing for me to do."

"But surely, you didn't come out just to work on your Dad's yard," Emma pointed out. "Didn't you come to spend time with him and Helena and your new sister?"

"I'm beginning to realize that now!" Amy agreed. "But, you know, since I got here, I've tried to fit in to the same role that I have back at Heartland – and then I've been feeling unhappy because I don't really fit in that way here. I've decided, though, that before I go I'm going to make a real effort to join in and become part of my new family." She paused. "The problem is, I don't really know how to go about it."

Emma looked thoughtful. "I understand how you feel, but I'm sure everything will work out before you leave." She gave Amy a reassuring smile.

"I hope so," Amy said and, as she smiled back, she realized that they had embarked upon the beginning of a friendship.

Later that evening, Amy prepared feeds for Spirit and Mistral before tracking Emma down in the tack room. She was piecing a bridle back together and she looked up as Amy walked in.

"I've prepared some more flower remedies for you," Amy said, holding out a bottle.

"Thanks," Emma took the bottle and placed it carefully on the shelf. "I've had an idea that might help you," she went on thoughtfully.

"Really?" Amy felt pleased that Emma was trying so hard to be friendly.

Emma nodded. "Why don't you offer to have Lily while your dad and Helena go out? It's their anniversary tomorrow," she said.

"It is?" Amy felt bad, that was something that she felt she ought to have known. It showed how little she knew about her father's new life.

"If you babysit then you'll be helping out Tim and Helena, but you'll also get to spend some time with Lily – maybe you'll get to know her better."

Amy thought Emma's plan over – and she had to agree that it seemed to be a good one.

During dinner, Amy noticed that conversation was a little strained. She felt awful as she remembered the way she had snapped at Helena when her stepmother had accidentally disturbed her session with Spirit. Helena was obviously doing everything possible not to ask about the gelding's progress and her brown eyes widened with astonishment when Amy brought up the subject by asking what she had enjoyed most about riding him.

She thought for a second before her face broke into a wistful smile. "It was the way he wanted to give me his all. It never felt like he was obeying me because I was the one in control, it was because we were a team and he wanted to contribute one hundred per cent to what we were doing."

Amy sighed. "I'm beginning to think Spirit is a one-woman horse. He's working well enough for me, but not in the way you're describing," she confessed.

"He didn't for me either in the early days. It was after his illness that he really bonded with me," said Helena.

"His illness?" Amy frowned.

"Yes, I remember the night well. The vet couldn't get out to us and we thought we were going to lose Spirit to a bad bout of colic," Tim explained.

"I spent all night in his box, nursing him – willing him to pull through," said Helena with a faraway look in her eyes. "I was afraid he wasn't going to make it. It was terrible to see him suffering. But I was determined not to give up on him, and he made it in the end. It was wonderful to see him fit and well again."

"I sometimes do that back at home," Amy said, beginning to realize that she might have more in common with Helena than she had thought.

The phone began to ring and Helena smiled apologetically as she went to answer it. Amy ate a mouthful of rice, but didn't really taste it. She was mulling over what Helena had told her. Now she could understand the level of devotion that Spirit had given to Helena after all her care. And suddenly she felt a great empathy with the beautiful gelding. *I'm not expecting him not to want to be with Helena any more. I just want him to give me a little of himself, too*, Amy thought, and immediately felt a slight churning in her stomach as she realized that she could apply the same thinking to her own situation with Helena. For the first time she realized that if she accepted Helena as a friend, it wouldn't detract from her loyalty and affection for her mother.

"Penny for your thoughts," Tim asked gently.

Amy glanced up and met his concerned gaze. "I'm just working through a few ideas," she smiled, realizing that all she had been doing for the last few minutes was pushing food around her plate.

Helena came back to the table and Amy suddenly remembered Emma's suggestion. "Have you got any plans for your anniversary yet?" she asked tentatively.

Tim looked a little surprised. "We didn't want to go out and leave you on your own – not with Lou away, too," he told her.

"No, no, you must go!" Amy exclaimed, "I'll be fine, and it's not like you get to go out often."

"I don't know that we'd be able to get a babysitter at such short notice," Helena put in, as she began to collect the plates.

"You don't have to worry about that," said Amy quickly. "I'll look after Lily. I'd love to. I haven't spent much time with her since I've been here and it would give us a chance to get to know each other."

Tim and Helena looked at each other. "If you're sure you don't mind..." Helena said slowly.

"That's settled then," Amy replied firmly.

Amy met up with Emma in the schooling ring the next day and gave the thumbs up sign in response to her raised eyebrows. "I'm on official babysitting duty tonight!" Amy told her.

"Great news!" Emma said, looking pleased. She was sitting lightly on Caspian in the centre of the ring. He was resting his hindleg and looked very relaxed.

"He's looking good," Amy observed happily.

"He is, isn't he?" Emma sounded proud.

"Let's see how he goes," Amy suggested.

Emma squeezed him forward on to the track and sent him into a balanced trot. She put him through all the paces and ended up by doing shoulder in. Throughout it all, Caspian kept a perfect outline and was relaxed and obedient. Finally Emma brought him to a halt and dismounted. Her cheeks were flushed and Amy smiled to see her so happy.

"He's so much more relaxed, Amy," Emma told her, "I never thought I'd see him like this."

"He's coming on really well," Amy replied. A thought struck her. "Now that you don't have to spend so much time concentrating on Caspian, I wonder if you could ride Spirit each day for me?"

"Sure." Emma looked at Amy quizzically. "But why?"

"He needs to go well for other riders as well as for me," Amy explained, but she didn't mention that Spirit had still shown no sign of breaking his bond with Helena.

Emma was too concerned with making a fuss of Caspian to ask any further questions. Amy felt a rush of delight as she watched, and hoped that her own breakthrough with Spirit would not be too far away.

Mistral was looking out over her door when Amy walked back up to the yard. As soon as she saw Amy she let out a long low whinny. Amy stopped and stared. Mistral had never called out to her before and she felt it boded well for their schooling session.

She tacked up Mistral before leading her out and slowly mounting her. Mistral shifted her weight slightly, but that was all. Amy squeezed her forward and Mistral obediently walked on. Amy rode her into the schooling ring where Emma was waiting with Caspian. "Will you give me a lead?" Amy called. "I'm sure that following another horse will really help Mistral. Just take it steadily."

Emma nodded and rode Caspian in front of Mistral. They

completed two circuits at a brisk trot and then Amy called for Emma to canter. In the next corner Emma sat deep into her saddle and sent Caspian into a smooth canter, which Amy followed. Mistral felt like silk, her neck arched proudly, and she was clearly enjoying herself. After one circuit, they slowed back to a walk and let the horses stretch their necks. As they did, there was the sound of someone clapping and they noticed Tim standing by the fence. "Well done," he called, crossing over to them. "They're both doing really well!" he exclaimed in delight. He reached up to give Emma's arm a quick squeeze. "You've worked really hard, and that was an excellent performance from Casp. I couldn't have done any better with him myself."

"It's all thanks to the remedies Amy gave me," Emma said, her cheeks turning red.

"No, it isn't," Amy put in quickly. "They're only effective combined with sympathetic handling – you've never given up on him, that's what's really brought him through."

"And as for Mistral, she's unrecognizable," Tim remarked, turning his gaze on Amy. "What you've done with her is amazing."

"Thanks, Dad," Amy felt a rush of happiness.

"Do you mind if I try her out?" Tim asked.

Amy hesitated. She wondered if it would be a little too much too soon for Mistral. But then, she realized, her father knew what he was doing. "Sure," she said, slipping down and helping him adjust the stirrup leathers.

Tim mounted lightly and squeezed Mistral forward. Mistral

laid her ears back at first and looked uncertain at leaving Amy and Caspian. But Tim maintained the pressure behind the girth and Mistral obediently stepped away. Amy watched her father's fluid movements in the saddle as he rode Mistral sympathetically. He trotted her in a serpentine, applied a half-halt and then sent her forward into a controlled canter.

"I could watch your dad ride all day," Emma commented, as they watched his expert handling of Mistral.

Amy nodded and felt a surge of pride, "My dad!" she said softly.

"Our cellphone numbers are written down here," Helena said, showing Amy. She smiled at Lily sitting quietly on Amy's lap. "Now, you be a good girl for Amy." She glanced up. "Oh, and Amy, I've suddenly remembered. We always leave her nightlight on. She gets frightened if she's in the dark."

Lily made a gurgling noise in her throat as if she was agreeing. Helena smiled and tucked a strand of Lily's hair behind her ear. "If you want anything, you'll have to call 'Amy' instead of 'Mum'. Can you say, 'Amy', Lily?"

Lily pushed her thumb into her mouth and gazed at her mother with a solemn expression.

"We'll be fine," Amy assured her, thinking how nice Helena looked. "You'd better go or you'll be late. Dad's already beeped the horn twice."

Helena smoothed a wrinkle out of her black dress, dropped a kiss on Lily's head and then hurried from the kitchen. "Thanks again," she called over her shoulder.

"Well," said Amy to Lily with a smile. "It looks like it's just you and me then."

Lily stared back at her through wide brown eyes that were just like Helena's. Strawberry jam was smeared around the corners of her mouth. "Let's clean you up," Amy said as she wiped it away. She breathed a sigh of relief when Lily didn't object.

"Now then," Amy went on. "How about some playtime and then a bedtime story?" She picked Lily up out of the chair and placed her on her hip, the way she had seen Helena do.

"Oow gone," Lily suddenly told her in solemn tones.

"That's right, Oow's gone away for a holiday. But she'll soon be back," Amy said brightly as she made her way up the stairs to Lily's nursery.

Helena had decorated the nursery herself. A mural was painted around three of the walls, showing a paddock full of horses grazing. On the fourth wall was a stable with a grey pony's head looking out over the door. Mobiles hung from the ceiling, there was a cuddly collection of soft toys sitting on a couple of shelves and the rocking chair next to Lily's cot held a stack of colourful picture books.

Amy sat Lily on a blanket on the floor and they spent some time playing with stacking rings and shape-sorters. After a while Lily began to yawn, so Amy gently placed her into her cot.

She tucked Lily in and selected a picture book to show to her sister. For the whole time that Amy turned the pages and talked about the pictures, she was aware that Lily hardly took her eyes off her. When she finally closed the book and smiled down at her, Lily smiled back. "Oow," she said quietly.

"Not Oow, Amy. Time to go to sleep now," Amy told her. She sighed as she clicked on Lily's nightlight, switched off the main light and left the room. She supposed she should be grateful that Lily had been good for her, but she couldn't help feeling a little dissatisfied. There was no denying that she still hadn't formed the kind of bond with her little sister that Lou had.

Amy wandered down to the kitchen and washed up Lily's dishes. Then she decided to make herself a coffee. She plugged the coffee machine into the wall and flicked on the switch. The room was instantly plunged into darkness. *The fuse must have blown and knocked out the trip switch*, Amy thought, wondering where the fuse box was.

Suddenly a frightened scream sounded from upstairs.

Chapter Ten

"I'm coming, Lily, hang on," Amy called as she felt her way through the darkness. She guessed that Lily's nightlight must have been on the same circuit as the kitchen lights. Her hands brushed against rough stone and she knew she must be going through the arch that led from the kitchen into the living room – which was also in darkness. She used the bookshelf and then the back of the sofa to guide herself to the bottom of the stairs. All the time she kept on calling reassuringly to Lily.

Once she was in the nursery she quickly made her way to the cot and grasped hold of Lily. She swung her sister up into her arms and rocked her gently until her crying stopped. A sudden surge of protectiveness took her by surprise.

"Amee," Lily hiccuped.

Amy felt her heart skip. "Yes, Lily, Amy's here. I've got you, you're going to be fine now."

Holding Lily close, Amy made her way from the nursery to Tim and Helena's bedroom. She flipped the switch and the lights came on – clearly they were on a different circuit. Amy set Lily down on the bed and then looked around. She remembered seeing a flashlight somewhere in the room and figured she could use that to find the fuse box downstairs. She soon spotted it on the mantlepiece and picked it up.

She turned back to Lily and felt a tug of emotion as the sight of her sister's tear-stained face.

"There now, the lights work in here. That's better, isn't it?" she said cheerfully to Lily.

"Amee," said Lily again, and she held her arms up, clearly wanting Amy to pick her up.

Amy quickly located the fuse box under the stairs and pushed the trip switch back up. Light filled the kitchen and the living room again – and Lily's nightlight sprang back to life, too. But instead of putting Lily back to bed, Amy fetched some of her toys and settled down on the sofa with her. "We've got a lot of catching up to do," she told her sister who beamed brightly.

Amy spent the next hour playing games with Lily and singing the nursery rhymes that she remembered her own mother singing to her. Eventually, Lily yawned and curled up against Amy who dropped a kiss on top of her curly hair. "My sister," she whispered, feeling for the first time in her stay the beginnings of a sense of belonging.

Amy was woken up by the sound of voices and, blinking the sleep from her eyes, she looked up to see Helena and Tim standing over her. "Hi," she yawned. "Did you have a nice time?"

"Lovely, thanks," Helena answered. "Wouldn't Lily go to sleep for you?"

Amy told them about the fuse blowing and then offered to put Lily back in her cot. After she had tucked her in, she made her way back down to the living room. Tim and Helena's voices were coming from the kitchen. She was about to join them but hesitated as she heard her name mentioned. She didn't want to eavesdrop, but it was difficult not to hear as their voices carried clearly through the arch. She heard her father say, "I think that Amy's been a little happier here these last few days – even with Lou away."

"Maybe that's helped," Helena put in. "Maybe Amy felt a little overshadowed by Lou."

"I don't see how," Tim mused, sounding puzzled. "Amy's always been so confident."

"So has Lou, from what you've told me, but didn't she feel the same way when you visited them both at Heartland?" Helena questioned.

Tim paused before he answered. "Yes, yes she did," he acknowledged slowly. "It was Amy and I who really clicked then."

"Maybe you've tried to overcompensate by paying less attention to Amy this time?" Helena suggested.

"If I have, it hasn't been deliberate," Tim replied. "But I do wish I could have spent more time with them both since they arrived."

"They understand how busy you are," Helena reassured. "You've got the business to run and the staff to look after – and that's on top of the time Lily and I demand," she laughed. "We all think you do pretty well."

Amy began to feel awkward, and was just wondering if she should go up to her room, when Helena spoke again. "And I'm sure that Amy and Lou appreciate all that you do. They're wonderful girls, Tim – you should be proud of them."

"I am." Amy could tell by the sound of her father's voice that he was smiling.

"I just wish I could connect with Amy a little more than I have," Helena went on. "I would love her to feel she can confide in me. I know I can never take her mother's place, I just want her to know that I'm here for her," she finished, sounding wistful.

"She knows. Just give her a bit more time. It's more difficult for her than for Lou. Amy was incredibly close to Marion," Tim explained.

Amy decided that she couldn't walk into the kitchen now. Instead, she quietly made her way up to her bedroom. As she lay down on the bed and rested her head on her arms, Amy felt everything was beginning to fall into place. The night's events had shown her that there was a bond between herself and Lily. She realized now that it had always been there, she just hadn't been aware of it. And Helena's words had opened her eyes, too. She was finally sure that her stepmother didn't want to interfere, but simply wanted to forge a good relationship with Amy and Lou. Amy felt bad for keeping her at a distance for so long.

As for Tim, Amy felt warm as she thought of her father. He loved her as much as ever; it was just that she hadn't fully recognized all the demands on his time. He clearly wanted to give one hundred per cent to everyone he felt responsible for, and that, Amy realized, meant a lot of people. During her visit, she had focused only on his relationship with her and, as a result, had felt that he didn't care enough. Now she had to admit to herself that she could have made more of an effort to spend time with him.

There was only one thing still troubling Amy – and that was

the fact that her father didn't have a photo of her on his desk along with the ones of Lou and Lily. Even as she thought about it, Amy felt her stomach churn a little. She closed her eyes and tried to push it to the back of her mind, determined to concentrate on all the positive things that had happened recently instead.

Amy spent the next few days divided between working with Mistral and Spirit, and riding out with Emma. She took Mistral for her first trail ride, with Emma on Spirit, and was thrilled at how much the big black horse was starting to enjoy being ridden. Each morning, when Amy came into the yard, Mistral would be looking over her door and would call gently the moment she saw her appear.

Her relationship with Lily was growing stronger every day and she made a point of spending an hour with her, and either Helena or Tim, each afternoon before tea.

The night before Lou was due to come home, Amy was in the kitchen rolling out playdough for Lily. She looked across at Helena, who was looking up a recipe, and decided to share the last worry about Spirit that was on her mind. "It doesn't matter how much I ride Spirit, or how many hours I spend doing T-touch on him, he still doesn't respond to me the way he did to you," she told her.

"I'm sorry, Amy, I just don't know what else to suggest," Helena frowned. "I feel so guilty that I disturbed your jumping the other day. I keep on thinking that I set your progress right back."

"It doesn't matter," Amy reassured her. "I've been doing some thinking and I've come up with an idea that I want to run past you to see what you think."

Helena turned to open the fridge and Amy noticed how pleased she looked.

"Do you remember when you told me about the time that you spent the night in Spirit's stall?" Amy continued.

Helena faced her, juggling an armful of lettuce, mayonnaise and eggs. "It was when he had colic," she nodded.

"Well, I know it's a bit of a long shot, but I thought that if I spent the night with Spirit, it might make him bond with me a little more. I know that the reason he formed such a strong link with you was because you helped him through his illness. I'm hoping that if I spent a similar amount of time with him, it might erase some of the dependence he has on you."

Helena went quiet for a while as she thought about it. "I can't see how it would do any harm," she said slowly.

"I thought I'd do it tonight," Amy told her.

"Well, I'll pack you a rug and a flask," Helena promised.

Amy chopped up a carrot stick and gave it to Lily to suck on. Lily took it and smiled up at her before banging it on the tray of her highchair. Amy forgot all about her worries concerning Spirit as she laughed at her little sister and thought how much she enjoyed being in her company.

Amy heaped a pile of fresh straw in one corner of Spirit's loose box and spread her rug over it. The box was warm and softly lit and Amy thought just how easy it would be to fall asleep.

She spent the first hour of the evening giving Spirit a thorough grooming. Spirit stood with his eyes half shut, resting his hind leg. By the time she had finished, Spirit's dappled coat gleamed and his mane and tail were like silk. Amy proceeded to crumble loose lavender powder into his coat and brush it through to encourage him to relax, just as she had shown Emma with Caspian. Finally, she massaged Spirit, moving in slow circles until her arms and fingers ached so much she had to stop.

Spirit let out a contented sigh as Amy settled herself on her bed of straw. She figured it must be the middle of the night as she let out a wide yawn. To keep herself from falling asleep, she softly began to sing old remembered rhymes from her childhood. *Why not?* she thought. *It helped me bond with Lily.*

As she sang, she began to remember the special times she had shared with her mother. Lately, Amy had often thought about the times she would miss sharing with her mom and the fact that her father hadn't been there for her childhood. But now she was realizing that she had had something special which Lou had missed out on – their mother's presence for all her childhood years. And, more than that, her mother had given her a gift, the gift of healing that Amy was now able to use to help horses – and sometimes people, too. She only had to remember all the people who had been helped through Heartland – all because of her mother's gift – and she immediately felt lucky. Amy closed her eyes and whispered a silent thank you to her mom, a thanks for the wonderful way she had touched her life in the time that she had been part of it.

***

Amy woke up to the feel of hot breath on her face and, as she sleepily opened her eyes, she found Spirit nosing her with his muzzle. She pushed him away gently as she sat up and stretched. Judging by the daylight streaming in through the cracks in the door, it was early morning. She got up and began to work her way through her stable chores. Soon she was joined by Emma.

"You look bushed," Emma observed, seeing Amy's tired expression.

"I've felt more awake," Amy admitted with a rueful smile.

"Listen, why don't you let me finish up here while you go and catch up on some sleep?" Emma offered.

"Thanks," Amy said gratefully. "I just need a quick nap to set me right and then I want to work Spirit."

"Do you think spending the night with him worked?" Emma asked interestedly.

"I hope so," Amy said, yawning as she headed slowly towards the house. *Even if it hasn't*, she thought, *it's done something for me, anyway. I've realized how lucky I am to have known my mom and to have had her touch in my life. It's something that Lou never really knew because she spent so much time at boarding school in England. She may have been lucky enough to have had my dad for a long time but I had Mom, and that's something special that will be with me for my whole life.*

There was no one up as Amy let herself into the house, and in no time at all she was crawling under her duvet. She closed her eyes, promising herself that she would sleep for just an hour. But she slipped into a deep, dreamless sleep until she was woken hours later.

"Wake up, sleepy head," said a familiar voice.

Amy groaned and realized that she had slept late and would have to rush to catch the school bus. "I'm coming," she mumbled and heard her sister laugh.

"And there was I thinking you'd be waiting outside with a welcome party for me," Lou declared.

"Whaa?" Amy sat up, looked into Lou's tanned face and suddenly realized where she was. "You're back!" she exclaimed hugging her. "Did you have a good time?"

"I had a fantastic time," Lou admitted, a slightly secretive smile playing on her lips.

"Good," Amy said and smiled back. She was puzzled by the expression on her sister's face. Her blue eyes were sparkling brightly and Amy instinctively felt that Lou was different in some way.

"What's going on?" Amy asked curiously. She tried to look serious, but the happiness radiating from Lou was infectious and she soon found herself grinning, although she didn't know why.

Before Lou could answer, Amy's attention was attracted by the sunlight glinting off her sister's hand. "Lou," she said slowly. "Am I going mad or is that a diamond ring you're wearing?"

"You're not and it is," Lou laughed happily.

Amy felt a great surge of exhilaration. "You and Scott are getting married!"

Lou nodded. "I can hardly take it in myself! Things have been going really well for us — and I knew that he wanted this time away to be special, but I never dreamed of a proposal." Her cheeks went pink as Amy stared at her, lost for words.

"Tell me how he proposed," Amy said finally. "I want every single detail."

Lou hugged her arms around herself and settled more comfortably on the bed. "Scott made me climb the whole way to the top of Ayers Rock to watch the sunrise. Just as the sun was appearing over the horizon, he asked me to marry him. Then he produced this fabulous champagne picnic from his rucksack and we just sat there and watched the rest of the sun come up." Her voice was soft, "I'll never forget it, never."

"Oh Lou, I'm so happy for you both!" Amy exclaimed excitedly. She felt a real joy inside her and her eyes filled with tears as she hugged her sister.

Lou hugged her back. "Enough about me. What about you? How've you got on without me?" she asked, the worry she had obviously felt apparent in her concerned gaze.

"Everything's turning out so well, Lou," Amy assured her. She told her all that had happened since she and Scott had been away.

"If I'd known how good this trip was going to be for us, I'd have suggested it six months ago!" Lou laughed.

Amy suddenly glanced at her watch. "It's one o'clock!" she exclaimed. "I've slept for hours."

"Well, you obviously needed it," Lou said practically. "Helena said you were awake for most of the night in Spirit's box."

"Well, it's the best news I've ever been woken up with, anyway," Amy said as she swung her legs off the bed. "You do realize we'll have to have a double celebration now? One here and one at home. Talk about forward planning on Scott's part!" She grabbed up her clothes. "Can you do me a favour?" Amy asked as she pulled on her clothes. "I've sort of forward-planned something myself today. Do you think you could get Helena down to the schooling ring in about half an hour?"

"Sure." Lou raised her eyebrows with curiosity. "Am I allowed in on the plan?"

"Better still if you come with her, and you'll get to see it in action," Amy called over her shoulder as she hurried downstairs.

Amy had memorized the dressage test that she had watched Helena ride on Spirit in the video. As she rode Spirit into the arena for a warm-up, she smoothed his neck. "Come on, boy, don't tell me that last night was for nothing," she murmured as she shortened her reins and asked for a turn on the forehand. Spirit executed it perfectly, but what was more, Amy got the distinct feeling that he wasn't just obeying a command from her, but was working as her partner.

She trotted and cantered him and there was no mistaking a sudden eagerness in his performance that she had never felt before. Gone were the almost lethargic movements. Spirit's paces were proud and elevated – he made Amy feel as if she was floating on air. His ear constantly flickered back to listen to her voice. His whole attention was focused on her, and she could almost hear him asking, *What next?*

But she knew that there was one crucial test that would prove whether she had been successful with Spirit. She glanced at her watch and then in the direction of the ranch, and her heart beat faster as she saw Tim, Helena, Lou and Scott coming down the path.

Spirit had noticed them, too, and he called out to Helena as she leaned against the fence. A frown crossed Helena's face – as if she wasn't too sure what Amy was planning – but Amy caught her father's eye and he nodded, as if to say he knew exactly what she was doing and he approved.

"OK, boy, don't let me down now," Amy said under her breath, as she squeezed Spirit away from the fence and into the centre of the arena. She halted in the middle and took a deep breath before putting Spirit into the first movement of the dressage test.

From the moment Spirit tracked right, Amy felt the difference in him. There was a channel of communication between them that simply hadn't existed before. He carried out the twenty-metre circles and three-looped serpentines in floating, elevated movements, all the while listening to her requests with his ear flicking back to the sound of her voice. When Amy finally halted, she felt a flood of happiness. For the first time, Spirit wasn't regarding her as a passenger, but as a partner that he respected and trusted and wanted to do his best for.

Ignoring the applause that burst from everyone watching, Amy rode into the second arena to put Spirit over a course of twelve jumps. Remembering the last time she had jumped

Spirit with Helena watching, she felt a little wary, but this time he wasn't distracted. As she finished the course, Amy knew she had participated in developing a horse that could well be a future Olympic champion. He had a soul that reminded her of only one other horse she had ever ridden – Pegasus. As her eyes sought out her father's, she knew by his emotional expression that he could see it, too.

He made his way across to her and reached up to place his hands over hers. "I've never seen you look more like your mother than when you were riding then," he said softly. "The memory of her will never fade for me while I have you. You have her spirit."

Amy felt her throat constrict and her eyes fill with tears.

"She would have been so proud of you," Tim finished, his voice husky from the strength of his feelings.

On their final day at the ranch, Amy, Lou and Tim rode out together. Lou stroked Mistral's neck as they walked three abreast along a wide track. "I just can't get over the change in her," she enthused.

"Just as I can't get over the change in you," Tim smiled. "Do you remember how reluctant you were to ride when I last stayed with you?"

Lou grinned. "It's taken me a long time to reach a point where I can honestly say I'm not afraid of horses any more, and it's all down to Amy."

"It's not," Amy protested, but she was thrilled to hear her sister's words.

"It is," Lou insisted. "You've always encouraged me and guided me and never made me do more than I was ready for."

"Sounds like the way you treat your horses," Tim smiled. "Talking of which, I've decided to give Emma the job of training the rest of my staff in your methods, Amy."

"Really?" Amy felt her heart skip with pleasure.

Tim nodded. "I've been so impressed with the results you've achieved here that it's convinced me it's the way forward with all my youngsters. If you can keep in contact with Emma – and maybe send her over some of your notes – it would be very helpful."

"Of course," Amy agreed happily. She and Emma had already promised to keep in touch – Emma was riding Spirit in a dressage competition in a couple of weeks and Amy was keen to hear how they got on. The girls had formed a bond that was growing stronger daily and Amy felt instinctively that she had made a friend for life.

Tim glanced at his watch. "We'd better head home," he said reluctantly, "or else Helena will send out a hunting party. After all, the barbecue can't start until we get back – not while I've got two of the three guests of honour!"

At the farewell meal that evening, Amy looked round at the same crowd that had gathered on her first evening at the ranch and reflected on how much had changed since then. *It's not just that events have changed, I've changed, too*, she thought. *I feel as if I've come to know myself better and gained a new perspective on things. I have so much going for me in my life – not just my work at*

Heartland. I have a bigger family now — Lou, Lily, Dad, Helena and Grandpa.

She felt a wonderful sense of fulfilment creeping over her. It was so good to know that she was leaving her dad's ranch with so many important areas in her life resolved. Even though she knew she would miss her new friends and family, she couldn't wait to get home and see everyone at Heartland again. She had missed them all so much. And one of the first things she would do, she promised herself, was ride out again on Sundance — hopefully with Ty alongside her. A soft smile touched her lips as she thought of Ty, and how supportive he'd been during her time at the ranch — helping her to find a new role for herself. Ty understood her so well and she knew he was always there for her, no matter what — even if it had to be over the phone rather than in person. He was a true friend.

Amy glanced up at the sound of a twig snapping on the ground. "Hey," Tim smiled down at her. "Mind if I join you?"

Amy moved along on her seat. "I was just thinking how lucky I am to have such a wonderful family and friends," she admitted. "I sometimes lose sight of that when I get wrapped up in my work."

Tim looked thoughtful. "I know what you mean," he replied. "There are always so many demands on your time that sometimes it's the people you love who end up missing out." He paused, looking into Amy's eyes. "I'm sorry I haven't been able to spend as much time with you and Lou as I would have liked."

"I felt a little left out to begin with," Amy confessed. "But then I began to realize that you have lots of people you are responsible for, and you're doing your best to give something of yourself to them all."

Tim looked struck by her words, "I've never really seen it like that," he said slowly. "I guess I'm too busy feeling guilty that I don't give more than I do. I know that I let you and Lou down badly in the years I wasn't around. I never want to let anyone down like that again..."

His voice tailed away and Amy instinctively reached out and took his hand. "We've had a wonderful time here," she told him. She hesitated, thinking about the photo of herself that had been missing from her father's desk.

As she was wondering whether to mention it or not, he placed his hand on her arm. "Are you OK? You seem a little too preoccupied for a party!"

Amy bit her lower lip. "I guess I was just a little upset the other day, when I was in your office. I noticed that you had photos of Lily and Lou, but none of me."

She glanced up to see a look of bewilderment flit across Tim's face. "But there is one of you," he insisted, sounding puzzled.

Amy shook her head. "No, there's not. There's one of Lou when she was little. And three of Lily together—" She broke off as Tim let out a laugh.

"One of those is of you – not Lily! The one of you holding your teddy bear. Didn't you recognize yourself?" he asked, smiling.

"No," Amy gasped, feeling surprised, delighted and

embarrassed all at once. Her cheeks burned. "I thought maybe you didn't want to have a photo of me when I was little because I had gone to live with Mom."

Tim surprised her by wrapping her up in a fierce hug. "I've never loved you any less because of that. Why would I? I love you just as much as I love Lou and Lily."

Amy nodded against his chest. It was wonderful to hear, even though she realized she had always known it deep down inside herself anyway. "I'm going to miss you," she said in a muffled voice.

Tim gave her a final squeeze before releasing her. "We'll all miss you, too. But it won't be long before we're together again – at Lou and Scott's wedding!" His eyes crinkled at the corners as his face lit up.

Amy nodded happily. She was beginning to realize that this time spent away from Heartland had allowed her to grow. She felt a surge of joy as she considered the times ahead, with the people she loved.

Holding hands, Amy and her father made their way back to where the rest of the family were waiting for them. Amy looked at their smiling faces. *You can't buy riches like these*, she thought contentedly. *Love is a gift – and it heals us all.*

Read more about Amy's world at

in book sixteen

Holding Fast

Amy was in different classes from Soraya for the rest of the day, but her friend's words stayed with her. She felt unsettled, and restless. Perhaps Soraya was right. Was it really a good idea to revisit the pain of the last few months, not knowing how it would affect everyone?

She tried to concentrate on her maths class, deciding that she would just have to wait and see. It was no good trying to guess how she'd feel until she'd met the horse and his rider for real.

At last the day was over, and Amy went to the parking lot. She spotted Lou's car and clambered in, picking up the map that Lou had placed on the dashboard.

"Where are we going?" she asked, unfolding the map.

"Venture's at a yard on the other side of town," said Lou as they turned on to the highway. "I think it's where police horses go when they retire, but it's where injuries and other problems are handled, too. Sounds interesting."

Amy took a deep breath and nodded, pushing aside her anxiety. It was interesting – another yard that treated horses, but only police horses. She wondered how different their approach would be. They might not use alternative methods of treatment at all; a lot of stables didn't. It would be fascinating to find out.

A tall, broad-shouldered man with short spiky dark hair was waiting for them at the entrance to the stables. Lou wound down her window. "Sergeant Garcia? I'm Lou Fleming, and this is Amy. We spoke on the phone."

Sergeant Garcia nodded. "Glad you could make it, Miss

Fleming," he said. "You can park just round to the left, by the stable block. I'll follow you up."

Lou drove slowly to where he had indicated, giving Amy a chance to look around. The yard was large and immaculately maintained, without a trace of loose straw on the clean white concrete. She caught a glimpse of a paddock on the right where four or five horses were grazing peacefully, and also a spacious training ring. Whatever techniques they used, Amy realized that Lou was right – as far as Venture's treatment was concerned, it would have to be a case of no expense spared.

Mark Garcia was standing by the stable block. There was something about his upright posture and his wide-set hazel eyes that suggested he was born to be a police officer. Amy appraised him silently. He seemed rather reserved, and it was difficult to see beyond his calm exterior. But he was welcoming enough, and as they walked around the stable block, he described what had happened on the night of the storm.

"I was on patrol out on the industrial side of town, and I'd nearly finished my shift," he explained. "The storm had blown up out of nowhere and I wanted to get Venture back to the stables. But then I heard some kids hollering from this breaker's yard."

He paused as if trying to recollect events as accurately as possible. "It turned out that the yard owner's son and some of his friends had got caught out in the storm. They'd tried to shelter in one of the old cars but a tornado whipped through the yard and turned it over."

Sergeant Garcia talked in a quiet, matter-of-fact way that

belied the drama of his words. But for Amy, the description brought back the full horror of the storm. She tried to block out the memories – the crack of the barn roof and the howling wind ripping through it – but they still made her shudder, and she clenched her fists tightly. As if sensing her feelings, Lou touched her arm.

Amy threw her sister a quick, grateful smile, then turned back to the sergeant. "Go on," she said, bracing herself.

"The kids were trapped. One of them was screaming, and the car didn't look safe. I called for help, but I knew something had to be done right away. So I dismounted, and led Venture towards the car."

A frown creased his forehead. "That's when things went wrong. A gust of wind got under a pile of tyres, and a couple of them crashed down on Venture's back. He went down on his knees, then scrambled back up right away. It all happened so fast that I wasn't even sure if he'd been really injured."

They stopped outside one of the stalls and Amy read the nameplate: VENTURE. It was a relief to come back to the here and now for a moment.

"Venture! Here, boy," called Sergeant Garcia. He clicked his fingers and a beautiful dark bay horse of about 17 hands appeared over the half-door. Amy's eyes took in his strong, stocky frame and noble head, then reached up to stroke his neck as the sergeant finished his story.

"His knees had a few cuts and he seemed shaken. I knew I shouldn't ride him until he'd been checked over, so I hooked his reins around my arm while I tried to help the kids. I managed to prise open the car door. Two of the lads scrambled out and they helped me wrench off the metal that was trapping the third. We got him out, but the poor kid was in a terrible state. It turned out he'd broken his leg in three places. I knew that moving him could have made things worse, but it was better than leaving him at further risk in that car."

"A tough decision," remarked Lou.

Mark Garcia gave a small smile. "Just part of my job," he shrugged.

Amy stroked Venture's soft nose. For all his size and strength, the horse had gentle features – a big Roman nose, large liquid eyes and a sensitive muzzle, suggesting a patient, willing character.

"What exactly were Venture's injuries?" she asked.

"The knee injuries were superficial, fortunately. His back's been more of a problem," said the sergeant. "He's seemed to be in pain ever since, but the vets can't seem to say why. He's been X-rayed and the bone structure is sound. There's a kind of stiffness about him, and he tenses up the minute anyone goes near him with a saddle – backs away and breaks into a sweat. No one can ride him." He paused, then added quietly, "Not even me."

Amy looked at him quickly. It was the first time the sergeant had given any indication of his feelings, or his attachment to Venture. But his face was still calm, and gave nothing away. "Are you riding a different horse on duty now?" she asked.

Mark shook his head. "We tend to work with one horse at a time. I'm on ordinary station duties until Venture's ready for work again. Makes a change, but I miss riding."

Amy stared at him. *I miss riding!* she thought. *Why not say, I miss Venture?* She could feel a tide of emotion welling up. Mark Garcia's description of the storm was vivid and accurate, and yet he somehow seemed detached from it. Suddenly Amy's heart reached out to Venture, the horse who was still suffering because of that terrible night. She knew how deep the damage could go, even if his rider didn't.

"Has Venture received any alternative treatments? Any kind of massage, herbs, anything like that?" asked Lou.

The sergeant shook his head. "No. We take a very straight approach here. But one of the vets had heard of Heartland, and suggested sending Venture to you."

For an instant, a hint of awkwardness showed in his hazel eyes, and was quickly masked. But it was enough. Amy read the look in a flash. *This wasn't his idea. He doesn't believe we can help!* she realized. Determination flooded through her. She would work with Venture, and help to heal the pain that conventional methods couldn't touch.

"Can we see Venture led around the yard?" asked Lou.

"Sure," said Sergeant Garcia. "I'll just get a lead rope."

He left Amy and Lou standing by Venture's stall. Lou scratched the horse's neck. "What d'you think, Amy?" she asked. "It's kind of tricky, isn't it, when he's had all these examinations already?"

"I think we should take him," Amy burst out immediately. "They haven't tried any alternative treatments. There's so much we can do for him." She saw the surprise on Lou's face, and controlled herself. "But we'll see what he's like when he's led in hand first," she added more calmly.

The sergeant walked with long strides across the yard and let himself into Venture's stall. The powerful horse stepped carefully through the door, watching where he placed his hooves as if he was walking on a treacherous surface. Sergeant Garcia walked him slowly up the yard and back again.

Amy watched the horse from all angles. There was no obvious problem – no limp, no unevenness in his stride. But there was a definite reluctance in the way he stepped forward, as though he was nervous – but nervousness wasn't quite the right word. As Sergeant Garcia had said, there was a sort of stiffness about him, a hesitancy in his movements even when he was just walking across his own yard.

Amy was curious, and the more she watched the gelding, the more her desire to work with him grew. She looked across at Lou and caught her eye, then gave a determined little nod. Lou looked doubtful, but nodded back in agreement.

Amy stepped forward. "I think we could work with Venture at Heartland," she said. She raised her eyes to Mark's, challenging him. "If you're sure you think it's worth it," she added.

Mark looked away from her gaze. "That's great," he said. "He deserves all the help he can get."

Lou talked through the arrangements with him. They agreed that Venture should be brought over to Heartland in a couple of days' time, on Saturday. Rather apologetically, the sergeant pointed out that there was likely to be a lot of media interest and possibly even a local television crew to film Venture's arrival.

"As long as they understand that we're a stables, not a zoo," said Lou. "And that the horses must be treated with respect."

"They're used to that from coming here," the sergeant assured her. "You don't have to worry."

With everything sorted out, Amy and Lou climbed back into the car and headed back to Heartland.

"I don't think the publicity can really do any harm, do you?" asked Amy.

"Well, like I said, we'll just need to make sure they go when they're told to," said Lou. "I hope they don't come pestering us on a regular basis."

"We had to deal with them before, when we had Gallant Prince," Amy pointed out. "It wasn't too bad then."

"True," agreed Lou. "But we managed to treat him successfully, remember? That made a difference."

"Well, I think we'll treat Venture successfully, too," said Amy. "I'll make sure we do."

At school the next day, Amy decided to use her lunch hour to check out more about police horses and their training, hoping it would give her some useful insights into Venture's problems. To her astonishment, her search quickly brought up more than she had bargained for. There was a whole series of articles about Sergeant Garcia and Venture – all much more dramatic than the brief account she had seen in the newspaper. "Police Horse Crippled For Life," ran one headline. "Nothing Ventured,

Nothing Gained – Police Officer Sacrifices Horse To Save Local Boys," ran another.

Amy skimmed through the articles. She was appalled at how much some of them twisted the truth. According to one account, the sergeant had ridden Venture at the car, and had managed to get the horse to kick the car door open to free the boys. It was crazy! And with a sinking feeling in her stomach, Amy suddenly realized that media attention alone wasn't the problem for Heartland. It was what they said. If reporters started over-dramatizing the work that she did, or got their facts wrong, it could do a lot of damage.

Amy took a deep breath. Venture was going to be a big challenge – but she was still certain that she had made the right decision. She thought once more of his big, noble features, and relived in her mind's eye the terrible moment when the tyres had crashed down on his back. If anyone could help a survivor of that night, it would be herself and Ty, at Heartland.